The Incredible RECORD SMASHERS

I shrugged and began typing.
"Come on, how hard can it really be
to get a world record?"

Sandesh looked at me like I'd suddenly
turned into a flying giraffe. "Lucy, world
records are extremely hard to achieve.
People spend their lives trying to master
their skills. You can't just get one."

To the incredible girls in my life:

My mum, a never-ending source of inspiration and material. My sister, Caroline, for always being there. And to my nieces, Penelope West and Amelia Pearson, and my goddaughter Penelope Parsons.

First published in the UK in 2021 by Usborne Publishing Ltd., Usborne House, 83-85 Saffron Hill, London EC1N 8RT, England, usborne.com

Usborne Verlag, Usborne Publishing Ltd., Prüfeninger Str. 20, 93049 Regensburg

Text © Jenny Pearson, 2021.

The right of Jenny Pearson to be identified as the author of this work has been asserted by her in accordance with the Copyright, Designs and Patents Act, 1988.

Cover and inside illustrations by Erica Salcedo © Usborne Publishing, 2021.

The name Usborne and the Balloon logo are Trade Marks of Usborne Publishing Ltd.

A CIP catalogue record for this book is available from the British Library.

ISBN 9781474974059   05683/1   JF AMJJASOND/21

Printed and bound in Great Britain by CPI Group (UK) Ltd, Croydon, CR0 4YY.

MIX
Paper from
responsible sources
FSC
www.fsc.org   FSC® C020471

We acknowledge Guinness World Records®
(www.guinnessworldrecords.com) as the original source
and copyright holder of the published details of all
Guinness World Records titles included in this book.
All Guinness World Records titles stated are correct
as of the time of printing, 2021.

The Incredible RECORD SMASHERS

JENNY PEARSON
Illustrated by Erica Salcedo

USBORNE

A message from the publisher:

Dear reader,

This book is about smashing records, which can be incredible and lots of fun. However, as you'll see, there are warnings in this book about some of Lucy's attempts, which do need to be taken seriously. **These things are not to be tried at home.**

If you do want to attempt your own record smashing, please turn to page 328 for top tips from the team at Guinness World Records on how to become a record smasher yourself.

CHAPTER 1

The largest screwdriver in the world is 6.32 m long and was made in India

The idea came to me after I was sent home from school on the last Wednesday of term for punching Billy Griggs on the nose. And even though he's the reason I had to miss the last two days of Year Six, I guess he's also the reason I ended up on a TV talent show in front of a live studio audience, asking the eighties pop star Paul Castellini if he'd like to help my mum. So if you were to say, "Lucy, do you regret walloping Billy's nose?" I'd say, "All things considered – it was probably worth it."

It was the day of our end-of-Year-Six presentations. We had to do a talk on a topic we were passionate about. Jack Perkins was up first, and he talked about the best football team in history, which, frankly, was always going to cause a massive argument. When Mrs Hunter finally got everyone to shut up by clapping her hands really loudly, she turned to Dylan Fry and told him he was next. But when he said he was going to do a talk about the *real* best football team in history, all the shouting started again. Mrs Hunter gave up on the angry clapping and instead yelled at us to be quiet. When eventually the noise had stopped, she did this massive sigh, muttered something at the ceiling about early retirement and then asked if anyone else wanted to go next. Sandesh raised his hand and started waving it about in a very eager way with his bum hovering above his seat.

Mrs Hunter did this big swallow, flopped down on her wheelie chair and said, "Okay, Sandesh, your go. I'm guessing this is on—"

And the whole class went, "**GUINNESS WORLD RECORDS**," in one big droney voice.

See, Sandesh has this thing about world records. Since he started in the summer term of Year Five, after he moved to Milton Keynes from south London, that is all anyone has heard him talk about.

For his presentation, he told us first that in India, where his grandparents come from and some of his relations still live, they have the **LIMCA BOOK OF RECORDS** and it is super popular. Then, after he had told us some facts about big stuff – big plants, big babies, big people – he told us about the longest ever fingernail. It belongs to one Mr Chillal, whose thumbnail measured 197.8 centimetres long or 6 feet 5.87 inches. Jack shouted out that that is the same height as England's best-ever goalkeeper, whoever that is – I wasn't really paying attention – but anyway, that started the football argument off again. And Mrs Hunter started with the angry clapping. Again.

After we had settled down and Jack had won himself a stretch in reflection (aka detention) at break time, Sandesh showed us a picture of the world-record-winning fingernails. They were truly disgusting. They looked like long twisty pork-crackling. Everyone made sick noises until Mrs Hunter told us we needed to be more mature than that if we were to survive when we went up to **Big School**. But kudos to Sandesh – he had definitely won the class over.

After Sandesh was Felicity Fairclough's talk on her favourite girl band The Megamouths and their lives, loves and heartaches. She didn't get too far before Mrs Hunter told her to stop because the content was too mature for Year Six. It was very difficult to understand the exact level of maturity Mrs Hunter wanted us to have.

When it came to my turn, I was truly excited to discuss mending electronics. Not to sound big-headed or anything, but apart from Sandesh, the other kids hadn't given me much competition. I took out my little toolbox and showed the class how to fix a broken games controller. Everyone was impressed. Mrs Hunter said, "That was very informative, Lucy," and she gave me an A grade and stuck a sticker on my top that said *Superstar*. And although stickers

8

aren't really for Year Sixes, I still liked it. Who doesn't want to be a Superstar?

But then, during questions, Billy Griggs stuck up his big hand and said, "If you're so good at fixing things, Lucy, why can't you fix your mum?"

His words hung in the air for a moment. My body reacted before my brain did and, in a flash, I was airborne and flying over the front row of desks. Later, when Mr Balls the head teacher read the report to me and Aunty Sheila, he said I had shouted, "Why don't I fix that smile right off your face with my **fiery fists of fury**?" They both agreed it wasn't a very "Lucy thing" to say, but secretly I thought it made me sound rather dangerously exciting.

Anyway, Billy and I ended up in a full-on fight on the floor. He's much bigger than me but I landed a punch right on his nose. We both felt the crack. We looked at each other for a moment, neither of us knowing what to do. But when the blood started pouring out of both his nostrils, Billy started bawling – and I mean really bawling. He said it was broken and he was going to sue me. Mrs Hunter grabbed a handful of wet paper towels, moved me out the way and pressed them on Billy's mashed-up face.

She told us all to sit down while she took him to the school nurse. I did as I was told and sat down at my desk and I noticed my hands were shaking. I think I was probably in shock as I'd never hit anyone before – I'm not really the punchy type. As he left, Billy shouted at me that he'd see me in court. That worried me, because I didn't want Mum getting upset about having a young offender for a daughter on top of everything else she seemed to be upset about.

Felicity, who was sitting in front of me, swung around and looked at me with these huge eyes and an even huger grin and said, "Oh my god, Lucy. That. Was. Just. So. Savage!"

I stared at an ink splodge on my shirt and growled, "Stop smiling at me."

She did not pick up on my mood at all. Instead, she clapped her hands together and said, "I can't, I just *love* all the drama!"

I didn't know what to say to that.

Everyone began whispering to each other and even though I really didn't want to cry in front of my class, my chin had other ideas and started to wobble.

Because I was trying to overpower my wobbly chin, it took me a second to notice that Sandesh had wandered up to my desk. I glared at him, but he didn't even flinch, he just said, "Do you know that Cecilia Bræjkhus, also known as the First Lady of boxing, has thirty-six wins from thirty-seven fights, and is **the longest-reigning female boxing world champion**?"

And I said, "Shut up, Sandesh." Which I totally feel bad about doing now, because I think he might have been trying to detract attention away from all my savagery.

He said, "Fine, whatever, Lucy." Then he put my glasses on my desk, which he'd picked up off the floor, and backed away with this wounded-looking face. And for some reason, I felt worse about that than the punch.

While twenty-eight pairs of eyes bored into me, I turned my glasses over in my hands. I hadn't even noticed that they'd fallen off in the scuffle. One of the arms was broken but I didn't mind that much as it meant I'd get to use my teeny-tiny screwdriver later. I'd won it in a cracker the Christmas after I'd turned nine. Mum had got a tiny plastic moustache in hers. She didn't take it off because I jokingly told her it suited her. Then she spent the rest of the day speaking in a Belgian accent and pretending to be Hercule Poirot, who is some TV detective I'd never heard of. But that was when she was well.

When Mrs Hunter came back, she made me take my sticker off my top and told me that someone from home was coming to get me. I really hoped it would be Mum who would be waiting for me at the school office, but it wasn't. I suppose I knew it wouldn't be really. Mum had been struggling again. She'd been sleeping so much. She probably wouldn't have heard the phone. Instead, it was Aunty Sheila standing there, with her pink hair and rainbow-coloured kaftan, looking all concerned.

After we'd listened to how disappointed Mr Balls was with me and that I was suspended for the last two days of school, Aunty Sheila gave me a big hug and told me that punching people in the face was something that I shouldn't do, even if the person really, completely deserved it.

It was on the car journey home that I realized something. And that something was that while Billy Griggs is a genuine, first-class birdbrain, he was right. Utterly and totally right. I'd read on the internet that people can get over depression, so why not Mum? And if I was so good at fixing things – which I absolutely was – then it really was up to me to fix her.

And in that moment, I decided I would. I just had to figure out how.

CHAPTER 2

The tallest dog ever is Zeus, a Great Dane who measured 1.118 m – which means he'd come up to Queen Elizabeth II's shoulders!

When I was littler, I used to have these nightmares about this black dog on our estate. They began after I started to notice Mum getting sad. I'd ask her what was wrong, and she'd tell me not to worry, it was just the black dog again. It might sound stupid now, but I used to think she was talking about an actual dog, or maybe even a ghost dog because I'd never managed to see it with my own eyes. What she was really talking about was her depression – she just didn't want to say that word out loud to me.

But before I properly understood what was going on, all I can remember thinking is that I had to do something about the dog. So I tried my best to hunt it down so I could ask it to go away, but the only dogs I ever saw were two cockapoos who were a bit full of themselves and a Jack Russell who had a massive attitude problem. Mrs Grover, who lives two doors down from us, has a big dog, but it's definitely more brown than black. I went round to check one day and accidentally got an eyeful of her playing badminton in her undies with Bob from the Co-op...but no black dog.

Every night before bed, I'd put out a cereal bowl full of dog food by our neighbour Mr Hannigan's back door. I thought the dog food, which I'd bought with my pocket money, might make the black dog go there instead of visiting Mum. I should say I don't feel brilliant that I did that to Mr Hannigan, but he doesn't even separate his recycling, so maybe he had it coming.

Even after I learned that the black dog wasn't real – that it was just a way people talk about depression sometimes – I still kept putting the dog food out.

I don't know why.

Maybe it was habit. Maybe it was because I didn't

know what else to do. Maybe it was because I had to do *something*.

And that's how I felt when Aunty Sheila pulled her van into our driveway that day after Billy Griggs said what he said: I had to do something. I had to fix my mum.

As we got out of the van, I could see that all our curtains were still drawn. Aunty Sheila tried knocking on the front door, but Mum didn't answer – to be honest, I wasn't expecting her to. Luckily, Aunty Sheila and I both have our own keys.

Aunty Sheila isn't my actual aunty. It's a hard-earned but much-wanted title, she says. I often end up staying at Aunty Sheila's for a few days when Mum's not well. The last time was a good few months ago though.

Mum and Aunty Sheila have been friends for ever. Mum says Sheila's the big sister she never had, even though they're the same age. They met when they were in the same class at primary school, which was way back in the last century. Mum says she was having trouble tying her shoelaces and Aunty Sheila helped her and that she's been helping her ever since. I'd love to have a friend like that. Really, Aunty Sheila's our only other family. Mum's an orphan – grown-ups can be those too, did you know? My dad might have walked out before I was born, but really, I'm very lucky to have a mum. Mum didn't have any parents when she was growing up.

As we got inside, Aunty Sheila flicked on the light in the hallway and said, "Lily? Lily, are you here? I've got Lucy with me. There's been a teeny punching thing at school today you should know about."

Mum didn't answer. I knew she'd be asleep. She could sleep all day when she was unwell.

"The school couldn't get through to you, so they called me about your daughter, the Littlest Rambo."

Still no answer.

Aunty Sheila rolled up her sleeves and said, "Let's put the kettle on, hey?"

I followed her into the kitchen, a little bit worried about what we might find. Let's just say that cleaning hadn't been Mum's top priority for the last couple of weeks. And it's never any priority of mine. Although I do try. Sometimes.

Aunty Sheila stopped short in the doorway and steadied herself against the door frame. "Oh, Lucy, is she bad again? Why didn't you say anything?"

I looked around at the unwashed cups and plates and the overflowing rubbish bin as though noticing them for the first time. It was pretty embarrassing.

"She's fine. It's fine. She's just been sleeping lots, that's all," I said – although we both clearly knew it wasn't fine. But I *needed* it to be fine, because if it wasn't, I knew what would happen – Mum and I would be separated again. Of course, I love Aunty Sheila and staying at hers is fine, good even, but I just want to be with my mum. That's how it's supposed to be. And, besides, how can you fix someone if they aren't even around to be fixed?

Aunty Sheila marched out of the kitchen and took the stairs two at a time. "Lily, are you awake?"

I followed her up and into Mum's bedroom. Mum was lying on the bed. Her face was so pale and strange, it was hard to look at her. She looked so small. Aunty Sheila grabbed my hand and said gently, "Lucy, wait outside, I need to talk to your mother."

18

But then Mum turned her face in our direction and said, "Is it morning already?"

Aunty Sheila let go of my hand and sat down on the bed and stroked Mum's hair, the way I wanted to but for some reason couldn't. And then she said, "My poor, poor, beautiful Lily. Do we need to get some help again?"

Mum began to cry. "Yes, I think I'd really like that." Then she looked at me and said, "I'm so sorry, Lucy, I'm just feeling ever so broken."

And I just stood there, as always, not knowing what to do. So I closed my eyes and remembered a good time, when Mum was well. It's what I do when I need to remind myself of who she really is and what she is like when she's happy.

I thought about all the mornings she'd wake me up by singing loudly about morning having broken and everything being beautiful. And she'd pull my duvet off me and say, "Up and at 'em, Lucy, my wonder!" Then I'd complain and tell her it was too early, so she'd jump into bed and kiss all the freckles on my face as she tried to count them and say, "What wonderful things are you going to do today, my love?"

And even though she hadn't asked me this time, I whispered to myself, "I'm going to fix you, Mum, I promise."

CHAPTER 3

The largest bunch of bananas contained 473 individual bananas and was grown in Spain

That night, after I bopped Billy on the nose, Aunty Sheila made me promise that in future I will always tell her when Mum gets bad. It was hard to explain why I hadn't said anything. I suppose I didn't want to admit it was happening again. That I hadn't been enough to keep Mum happy. I think a tiny part of me was embarrassed too. That we were living like we were.

After Aunty Sheila had kissed me goodnight I tossed and turned on the mattress in my canoe. I should explain, the canoe is what Aunty Sheila considers acceptable as a guest bed for when I stay at her house. She says I can dream I'm sailing off on an adventure every night. But I don't really dream and definitely not about adventures. And that night, all I could think about was Mum's pale face and how small she seemed. Billy Griggs's words kept ringing in my head. I *should* be able to fix Mum. I just had to find a way.

But never in a million gazillion years did I think it would end up with me making a right show of myself on **national TV**.

The first morning after the savagery unleashed by my **fiery fists of fury**, Aunty Sheila burst into her living room singing Beyoncé's "Single Ladies" and waggling her bum about very enthusiastically. She was wearing a yellow jumpsuit and a brown headscarf tied up in her

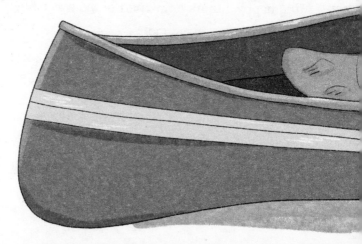

hair and she looked like the most wonderful banana I had ever seen.

She plonked herself down on top of my sleeping bag, and even though I was worried she might flatten my internal organs, I didn't really mind because she squashed some of the sadness out.

"No worries today, okay? Your mum is where she needs to be, and you are where I need you to be, and that is right here with me. Okay?"

"Okay."

"We'll all get through this. We always do."

I nodded but, really, I was done with just getting through it. I wanted to fix it.

"How about we spend today mending some things?" she said, stroking my cheek. "Would you like that?"

And even though I knew she wasn't strictly talking about Mum, I said, "More than anything."

Aunty Sheila used to work in the city, stocking and sharing things, but then one day she said she'd done enough of that and quit. Now, to make money, she spends every Sunday at car boot sales. She collects broken things, fixes them and sells them on. She's the one who taught me my excellent fixing skills. She showed me how, if you take something apart and look ever so carefully, it's usually easy to spot what's out of place. It's just a question of effort and time. Aunty Sheila says most things can be fixed, it's just people are too quick to throw stuff away.

For breakfast we had cereal that looked like it had been scooped up from the bottom of a hamster cage. Aunty Sheila has been waging a war on sugar for as long as I can remember. For some reason she thinks it's dangerous. I asked her how much damage a bowl of HoneyChocopufflepuffs could actually wreak. She fixed her eyes on me and whispered, "Unimaginable damage, Lucy," and then launched into a long talk about underperforming pancreases and irritable bowels, which I tried my very best not to listen to.

After my jaw became too tired to eat any more, we headed down to my absolute favourite place in the world: Aunty Sheila's shed. It's not your usual shed, because she has reinforced the walls and stockpiled food and medicines there in case of an apocalypse. I should explain this too: Aunty Sheila is a catastrophizer. She didn't tell me this – I found out myself by googling. A catastrophizer is someone who worries that everything is going to end in some big disaster.

We used to make fun of her for being like this, but then the global pandemic hit and she was the one who had the last laugh. She was very *I told you so* about the whole thing and had us eating tinned peaches and crab paste, while everyone else was battling for online deliveries. Aunty Sheila keeps the shed well-stocked at all times. She says those who fail to prepare, prepare to fail. She reckons three people could survive in our shed for a whole year if the worst happened. I asked her what could be worse than a global pandemic and, to be honest, she was a bit vague. But in any event, we're sorted if we ever have to hide away during a surprise zombie invasion or an attack from warmongering space aliens, and *that's* always reassuring.

Aunty Sheila held up an old alarm clock in one hand and a camera in the other. "What do you want to work on?"

I sat down on a crate containing three hundred tins of sardines. "I'll take the camera."

"Good choice. You fix that and it will make us a few quid on Sunday."

I set about opening up the back of the camera and Aunty Sheila took the face off the alarm clock. Even though she was trying to look like she was concentrating on what she was doing, she kept snatching glances at me. I knew what was coming.

"You know, kiddo, I spoke to your mum last night and her doctors think...no, we *all* think—"

She didn't need to say any more. "I'm going to stay

here for a bit, aren't I?" I tried really hard to keep my voice from wavering.

"You okay with that?"

It didn't matter if I was or wasn't. It had happened enough times for me to know it was pointless to try and argue.

"Can I speak to her?"

"Yes. Soon. Maybe in a few days."

I didn't look up. I knew the systems that had been put in place for when Mum got sick, but I'd only ever stayed at Aunty Sheila's for three or four days max before. Something told me that this time was going to be longer. "How bad is she?"

"There's nothing about your mum that's bad, Lucy. You know that. She just needs some time – to have her feelings and move through them. She's in a special hospital for people who are having a hard time. They're going to take great care of her there, I promise."

My screwdriver jolted off the screw I was working on. I was so over Mum *having feelings*. She should just be happy, like everybody else. Or pretend to be, like I did. I didn't say any of that to Aunty Sheila though. I just said, "It's fine," and made my own promise that I'd work on the plan and fix my mum as soon as possible.

Luckily, that plan came to me three days later at the car boot sale.

CHAPTER 4

The creature with the most powerful punch in the animal kingdom, striking at a force one hundred times its weight, is the mantis shrimp. I think that's probably even more powerful than me!

On Saturday morning I woke up to find Aunty Sheila standing over me wearing a pair of bright orange overalls and a gas mask. In her hand she was brandishing a can of Febreze.

I really wasn't in the mood for one of her drills, so I scooched down to the bottom of my sleeping bag and told her I was asleep.

"Gas in **five**."

"I am very fast asleep, Aunty Sheila."

"Five...four..."

"Please, can we do this later, when I'm not my most fully asleep?"

29

"That's a lot of backchat for a supposedly unconscious person. And you don't get to choose when there's a gas attack. **Three...two...**"

I popped my head out of the sleeping bag. "I can't get my gas mask because I'm absolutely completely fast asleep."

"**One**." She sprayed the Febreze in my direction. "And you're dead."

"Good, will you leave me alone now?"

She pulled her gas mask up on top of her head and jabbed the can of Febreze at me. "Gotta be better prepared than that, kiddo."

"Prepared for what? Air that smells like lavender and patchouli?"

"You'll thank me when you've survived an unexpected chemical attack. It's all about preparation."

It was difficult to argue with that reasoning.

She swept out of the living room into the kitchen, announcing, "And now, we breakfast."

I scrambled out of my sleeping bag, climbed out of the canoe and trudged my way into the kitchen, where Aunty Sheila was serving up more hamster-cage scrapings into two blue bowls.

She set one down in front of me and said, "Don't snarl at your food."

I growled at the bowl ferociously and her big red lips stretched across her face. "Oh, I forgot to say. As it's officially the start of your summer holidays, I've invited a friend round for you to play with."

"You have?" I didn't like the sound of that. I was far too old for playing, and besides, I didn't have time for a friend when I had a mum to fix. "Who is this *friend*?"

She tightened the straps on her orange dungarees. "The old couple who live next next door—"

"Old people?" Why would I want to play with old people?

"Not them. They've got their grandson staying with them for the summer. His parents have to work – touring America or something. Anyway, I said you'd love a play date. He's an only child, like you – I thought you might like someone your own age to hang out with while you're here."

"A play date? You said I'd love a *play date*? I'm not in reception. I'm not four years old!"

"He's coming over at ten once he's finished his piano practice."

I scowled.

"Don't look so grumpy."

At exactly ten the bell rang and me and my grumpy-looking face opened the door to reveal an exceedingly happy-looking face.

"Sandesh? *You're* my play date?"

He frowned ever so slightly but his smile didn't fade when he said, *"Play date? We're not in reception, Lucy."* Then he shoved a bag of pink shrimps in my hand – the sweets, not the freshwater-prawn type. If it hadn't been for my dangerously low blood-sugar levels from Aunty Sheila's miserable diet, I would not have accepted them. As it was, I stuffed them in my back pocket and his grin got even wider.

I set him straight. "It's not a play date and I know we're not in reception."

"I know! Can you believe we've finished Year Six? Actually, did you officially finish Year Six? You missed the last bit because you broke Billy's nose." He was *still* smiling when he said all that.

"Yes, I finished Year Six," I said a bit crossly, even though I suddenly wasn't sure if I had. I'd have to check with Aunty Sheila later. My stomach did this weird little wobble at the reminder of what I'd done. "It was definitely broken then – Billy's nose?" I'd suffered a significant amount of remorse since my afternoon of savagery. I felt awful about what I'd done and also sad I'd missed my very last days of primary school.

"That was the rumour, but it looked pretty much back to normal when Billy came in the next day, so I don't know how true it was."

Noses were obviously much easier to mend than mothers.

Aunty Sheila called out from the kitchen. "Don't make the poor boy stand out there on the front doorstep like a door-to-door salesman, invite him in!"

"Come on then." I stepped to the side and Sandesh walked right into the kitchen and up to Aunty Sheila and shook her hand like he was closing a business deal.

"You're a very lovely shade of orange today, Ms Stafford."

Aunty Sheila positively beamed and said, "Why thank you, Sandesh, I do like a bright colour! But do call me Sheila."

Since when is *orange* a compliment?

"That's a very...interesting hat you're wearing," he continued.

"Not a hat, Sandesh. A gas mask."

Sandesh nodded. "I understand."

What did he mean? How could he understand? I knew why she had it and I still didn't understand.

Aunty Sheila threw her gas mask into the fruit bowl and made her way out the side door. "We're going to be doing some fixing today, ready for tomorrow's car boot. Would you like to join us?"

"That would be great, if that's okay, Ms Stafford, I mean Mrs Sheila. Sorry, I mean Sheila."

And before I knew it, I was sitting on sardines fixing things with Sandesh in *my* special shed, when I really should have been working on a way that I could help Mum. To be honest, I was very huffy about Sandesh being there. I thought he was going to keep going on and on about **world records**, that he'd get in my way and stop me from doing what I needed to do. I was wrong about that though, I guess. Actually, in the end, I was wrong about a lot of things.

CHAPTER 5

The most expensive postage stamp is the British Guiana 1c Magenta, which sold for a whopping £5,588,577. Wowsers!

While Sandesh stood looking around the shed with his mouth open, I rummaged in my toolbox and continued working on my camera. It was taking me longer than I'd expected to mend it. I had tried everything I could think of, but it still wouldn't work. It was giving me the jittery-panics. I had to be able to fix things. I just *had* to.

"Wow! There's a lot of stuff in here." Sandesh let out a low whistle. "Why don't you just sell all this stuff online?"

Aunty Sheila slowly lowered the old lamp she was rewiring and trained her gaze on him. "We don't talk of such things in this house, Sandesh."

Sandesh's brow crumpled. "What things?"

"Online selling," I explained. "It's a long story which basically comes down to her lack of attention."

Aunty Sheila rolled her eyes. "It was a moment of learning, Lucy. We could all do with paying a little more attention. Do you know, Sandesh, I once bought what I thought was a beautiful, brightly-coloured Andy Warhol print of our Queen? Something I had coveted for years."

"I didn't know that, Ms St— Sheila."

"And do you know what that much-coveted print turned out to be?"

"Not a clue."

I smirked. I'd heard the story a gazillion times before, but Aunty Sheila's unwavering fury never got any less funny.

"It turned out to be a first-class stamp. Yup, that's right; one you get from the post office."

Sandesh shook his head. "A stamp?"

He was making a properly good show of being dismayed for Aunty Sheila, but I could tell there was a flicker of a smile on his lips.

Aunty Sheila pointed her screwdriver at him. "And that, Sandesh, is what can happen when you buy things *online*."

"I understand," Sandesh said, but his crumpled forehead made me doubt that he did.

"You've got to see things up close to appreciate what they really are," Aunty Sheila went on. "You can't always believe the descriptions others provide. You've got to read the small print. You've got to pay attention and work it out for yourself."

"A bit like you have to do with people," I muttered. I'd heard this talk before too.

She smiled at me. "Yes, Lucy. A bit like you have to do with people."

"That was a very inspiring talk, Sheila," Sandesh said, then gave me the smallest wink, as though he knew what it was like to be preached at repeatedly.

Aunty Sheila can't have noticed the wink because she nodded her appreciation and said, "Thank you, Sandesh."

We were all quiet for a moment. I fiddled some more with my camera and wondered what Mum might be doing.

And then Sandesh said, "But do *you* know, Sheila, the world record for the **most expensive item ever sold on eBay** is a yacht for $168 million," which made me chuckle.

Aunty Sheila turned back to her lamp. "Don't get much call for those at the car boot, Sandesh."

Later, without bothering to check with me, Aunty Sheila asked Sandesh if he wanted to stay for lunch. He was well up for the idea. He said, "I'd love to!" very enthusiastically, even though she had told him that we were having some weird aubergine and buckwheat dish. I mean, who willingly agrees to eat that? It made me miss Mum's cooking – in my opinion, there's nothing wrong with fish fingers, chips and beans. But Sandesh made a good show of enjoying Aunty Sheila's weird concoction, even though it was truly awful – sludgy and gritty at the same time. I've got to give it to her, she has an alarming talent for making unimaginably horrible food. It does make me wonder if it would actually be worth bunkering down in the safety shed with her when the apocalypse comes. It might be better to take my chances with the nuclear weapons.

Over lunch, Aunty Sheila went on to invite Sandesh to join us at the car boot sale the next day. I was being completely ignored in any decision-making processes so, I admit it, I had a bit of a sulk. But when Sandesh said, "That sounds AWESOME!" he sounded so exceptionally happy that I couldn't stop the smile curling on my lips. I didn't want him to see it though, so I shovelled in some aubergine-sludge and mumbled that he'd have to be up really shockingly early and he probably wouldn't like it anyway.

But he said, "I'll check with my grandparents, but I reckon I can convince them. And I always get up early."

I wasn't surprised by that – he did strike me as the perky up-with-the-birds sort.

Aunty Sheila said, "Super! Be here at 6.30 a.m., Sandesh, and you can help me strap the canoe to the roof of the van."

"She's been trying to sell the canoe for over two years," I told him.

"Tomorrow will be the day when it finally goes, I just know it."

I had mixed feelings about that. "Where will I sleep if you sell the canoe?"

"We'll think of something."

I had been hoping she'd say a bed, but I saw her eyes flash to a box of **giant inflatable flamingo rings** she'd been storing under the stairs. I caught her eye and shook my head. She just did this tinkly laugh and said, "The tingles in my bones are telling me that this is going to be a very good car boot."

Sandesh said, "I reckon so too. I'm well excited!"

"Are you now?" I said.

"Yeah – course!"

And then he hesitated and said, "But what exactly is a car boot?"

Unbelievable!

"What do you mean, *What exactly is a car boot?*"

Aunty Sheila gave me one of her scowls. "Don't be so rude, Lucy. A car boot, Sandesh, is where people gather together in a field and sell things they no longer need from the boots of their cars. It can be quite lucrative."

I hadn't seen any evidence of car boots being that much of a money-spinner – and I'd been to at least a hundred with Mum and Aunty Sheila – but I didn't argue. I didn't have the energy.

"It sounds great," Sandesh said. "I reckon it could be an adventure."

I think my top lip did an involuntary snarl when he said that, because at the time, with my head full of thoughts about Mum, I couldn't see how a car boot could be that exciting. Which shows how much I knew!

CHAPTER 6

The oldest competitive canoeist is seventy-seven-year-old Avis Noot from the UK. Go, Avis!

I spent the rest of the evening working on the camera, which was (very annoyingly) behaving like it didn't want to be fixed, and trying to dodge Aunty Sheila's concerned eyes and questions about how I was feeling. I didn't want to talk about how I was feeling. In fact, I didn't really want to talk at all.

When I woke up the following morning I had kind of forgotten that Sandesh was coming to the car boot, so it was a bit of a shock to discover him standing over my canoe, smiling his usual massive smile at me.

"Rise and shine! It's car boot day! Do you know that the **world-record car boot sale** involved two thousand cars and was held in our nation's capital in 2007?"

Frankly, it was far too early for world records, so it was difficult to muster any enthusiasm for this rather uninspiring fact. I reached for my glasses and put them on. "No, Sandesh, I was not aware of that. I'm afraid you might find Totternhoe's car boot sale a little less impressive."

"Don't be such a downer. I'm sure it will be magnificent."

Aunty Sheila burst into the room. She had a huge green scrunchie in her hair and was wearing her yellow jumpsuit again, which made her look a bit like an oversized pineapple.

Sandesh and I both looked her up and down and he said, "You are looking very...exotic this morning, Sheila."

I don't know what passes for a compliment these days, but Aunty Sheila seemed to like it because she waved her hand dismissively and said, "Oh, Sandesh, such a polite young man. Would you like some breakfast?"

"I'd love some breakfast."

"Wonderful, you can try the yoghurt I've been making."

My stomach sort of contracted into itself. "You've been making your own yoghurt?! Why? What's wrong with a Müller Fruit Corner?"

"My yoghurt is truly something special. It helps introduce good bacteria into your gut. Improves your biome."

"I have absolutely no idea what you're talking about."

"Trust me, it's delicious."

It was not delicious. Fizzy yoghurt should not be a thing.

We headed off to the car boot in Aunty Sheila's van. I was not at all happy that Sandesh got to ride shotgun and I ended up in the back wedged next to a box of glittery loo seats.

But things began to get better, because when Sandesh and I were moving all the junk onto the stall, the idea of how to fix Mum finally found me. It's funny how that can happen – you worry about how to solve a problem and then the answer falls into your lap, like you were destined to find it.

Aunty Sheila had gone off for a browse round the other stalls before all the customers came. She'd seen a full Sylvanian Families set and had become so excited that her green scrunchie began to dance around on the top of her head.

While she was off being convincingly out-haggled, Sandesh and I started to display a box of random stuff on one of the trestle tables. As Sandesh was telling me that the world record for **the longest ear hair** is 18.1 centimetres and I was trying not to bring up my fizzy yoghurt imagining it, I picked up a hardback book about garden birds and a photo dropped out onto the grass. Right by my feet.

I stood there, looking at these two faces staring back at me. I don't know why, but it immediately made me want to cry. Sandesh must have noticed something was up, because he stopped right in the middle of telling me about **the world-record longest nipple hair** (a staggering seventeen centimetres, if you're interested) and he said, "Lucy, is everything okay with you right now?"

I bent down and picked the photo up. "Yeah, it's just a picture of my mum, that's all."

But it wasn't *just* a picture.

My voice got stuck somewhere between my tonsils and the other dangly bit at the back of my mouth and I only managed to whisper, "She just looks so completely happy."

Sandesh simply said, "I understand." And you know what? I think he did.

The photo must have been taken quite a while back. Probably when Mum was working as a hairdresser in London. It was her, but she looked so different, so beautiful. It wasn't all the blue make-up on her eyes, or her bleached blonde hair. It was the fact that her smile flickered across every part of her. From the freckles on her nose to the tips of her outstretched fingers – her whole body was smiling. This was the mum I wanted.

She had one arm around a man with very green eyes and a silver cross dangling from his left earlobe.

I turned the photo over and looked at the back. Written in black ink were the words, *You are my happiness*.

I felt this weird sensation bubbling up from the pit of my stomach which I was certain was not yoghurt-related. For, in that instant, I was convinced I knew the answer to finding Mum's happiness: it was this man with eyeballs that looked like he had taken them out and polished them.

I became aware of Sandesh hovering at my shoulder. I held up the photograph – I wanted him to see it. "Look, Sandesh, this...*this* is my mum."

I wasn't sure what I was expecting, but his reaction was entirely surprising. He started to breathe very quickly and began fanning himself with his hand. He even started hopping from foot to foot.

"Do you know who that is, Lucy?"

I looked at him for a moment, trying to work out if he was being serious. "Yeah, I just told you, it's my mum."

"I am not talking about the woman." He pointed at the shiny-eyeball guy. "I'm talking about him."

"Him? Do you know him?"

"Yes, I do!"

And I grabbed his shoulders, possibly a little too firmly, and said, "Tell me everything, Sandesh. Tell me everything, now!"

CHAPTER 7

The most expensive mobile phone sold for £675,123

Paul Castellini was apparently a late-eighties icon, famous for three chart-topping hits...and Sandesh's favourite pop star. It is *so* like Sandesh to love music by someone who wasn't even born in this century.

Paul's musical back-catalogue wasn't the only reason Sandesh was so excited. He was also hopping up and down because Paul Castellini had recently been announced as the head judge on a new TV show called **RECORD SMASHERS**, where contestants would go on and try to break world records. This show, Sandesh said, was absolutely going to be the best thing on TV.

Sandesh was hanging onto the photo and I had to

tug quite hard to get it back out of his hand. Once I'd prised it from his grip, Sandesh looked at me with big wide eyes and said, "He's not your dad, is he – Paul Castellini?"

I laughed. "No, my dad is called Neville and last I heard he was living in Truro. Paul Castellini must have been a friend of my mum's. A really good friend – look how happy they look together in this photo!"

"Your mum was friends with **THE Paul Castellini**? Wow! He's an actual musical legend, Lucy. He doesn't even do interviews. He's known for being a man of mystery – and your mum knew him! I can't believe it!"

I couldn't believe it either.

For in that moment, I knew.

I'd found the answer to Mum's happiness. And the answer was Paul Castellini.

It said as much on the back of the photograph. I turned it over in my hands and whispered the words, *"You are my happiness,"* to myself, and somehow, it felt true.

I decided there and then that I'd stop at nothing to get Paul Castellini and Mum together again. He'd make her happy and she'd be the mum in the photo. My mum.

I felt the crackle of excitement in my belly. This really was the most excellent news. The fact that Mum's happiness was linked to a famous person was going to make fixing her so much easier, or so I thought. All I had to do was find out Paul Castellini's number, phone him up and ask him round ours for his tea. And then maybe together, we'd be able to get rid of her depression. It seemed like a foolproof plan.

I was starting to go over the details in my head when Aunty Sheila came back and rudely interrupted me. She was carrying a massive box of tiny Sylvanian squirrels and told us now was our chance to have a look around the stalls. She gave us both a fiver, as thanks for helping out on the stall.

I wasn't bothered about shopping, but Sandesh was desperate to browse, so, with my mind whizzing with plans and possibilities, I agreed to show him around. To be honest, all I wanted to do was go home and start my Paul Castellini investigation. But Sandesh, well, he seemed to be having the time of his life, even though I was practically dragging him along by his elbow. I was hoping that if we moved fast, time would pass quickly too, but he wanted to stop and look at everything!

"You are looking…rather joyous," he said as I swung him round a stand of faded leather jackets.

"Joyous?" I hadn't meant to. I'm not one for flashing my feelings about for everyone to see.

"Yeah, you don't smile much usually."

"Well, compared to you, no one smiles that much."

He tilted his head. "I suppose that's true. My mum says that people don't always like to wear their happiness on the outside."

"Maybe not everybody is as happy as you or your mum, Sandesh."

"But you seem happy right now?"

"I've just had a bit of good luck, that's all."

He suddenly stopped still next to a stall selling old electronics equipment. "Talking of good luck…look at that!"

I scanned the table but I couldn't see anything *that* exciting. "At what?"

"This!" His eyes flashed excitedly as he picked up an

old-looking mobile phone. "I've always wanted my own phone."

"You're going to need a phone if you want to survive Year Seven."

"Mum and Dad aren't keen. I thought, because they're touring more, they might get me one to stay in touch – but they think they're dangerous!"

"How in the world can a phone be dangerous? That's so daft," I said (which seems ironic now, considering everything that happened later). "And where are your parents anyway?"

"America. Mum's a classical pianist. Dad's her manager. She's quite famous – in classical music circles anyway."

As I have zero interest in classical music and highly doubted that any piano player could be famous, I think I may have completely ignored everything he said and turned the conversation back to the phone. "Do you think you want to buy it then?"

Before he could answer, a man with a flat cap and big fluffy eyebrows said, "That's nine quid that, son."

"You're kidding – that's way too much." Sandesh looked at the phone and did this big dramatic sigh.

I took it from him and examined it, to see if it was worth the money.

Flat-cap man's fluffy eyebrows rammed together like two duelling caterpillars. "Well, don't you be thinking of nicking it, girlie. 'Cos if I don't catch you, the Old Bill will. Police have been crawling around here today."

Sandesh gasped, looking truly offended on my behalf. "Lucy would never steal anything. She's a very good person, *actually*."

I think I might have blushed. I quite liked being called "a very good person, actually". Especially by Sandesh, because he *is* a very good person and I didn't think he'd think I was one.

Sandesh lowered his voice and said, in a surprisingly threatening way, "Yeah, a very good person – when she's not breaking noses, that is."

Flat-cap looked me up and down, as though he was assessing how dangerous I was – which I also quite liked, to be honest. Sandesh's words had given me oodles of confidence and I decided I wasn't going to let anyone accuse me of being a criminal. So I eyeballed the guy and said in my most determined of voices, "We're good for the money," and I held up my fiver as proof. "Now tell me, does it work?"

He looked a little taken aback and muttered, "Needs a new battery, I think, and a new screen."

Easy enough stuff to fix. I gave Flat-cap my steeliest stare. "We'll give you seven quid for it."

He rubbed his eyebrows. "Eight pounds and I'll throw in a case."

"Done."

I handed my fiver over to the guy and nodded at Sandesh to do the same.

Sandesh handed over his fiver and said, "I can't let you do this, Lucy!"

"Relax, Sandesh. I'm only giving you three quid for an old phone, not $168 million for a superyacht."

"Roman Abramovich might have a pretty awesome yacht, but I doubt he has a friend as great as you," Sandesh said, right before leaning in to hug me.

I took a step back. "You, Sandesh Agrawal, need to calm yourself right down."

Sandesh must have realized he'd gone a bit over-the-top because he said, "I understand." Again.

When we got back to our stall, Aunty Sheila was in a right flap. "Where've you been?" she demanded, which was a stupid question because she knew exactly where we'd been.

I answered her anyway. "We've been looking at the stalls."

"Did you not see all the police? Apparently a couple of inmates have escaped from the nearest prison and have been spotted in this area. I'd never forgive myself if you were murdered by a convict."

I appreciated Aunty Sheila's concern, but really, how likely was it that I'd meet my end in broad daylight at Totternhoe car boot sale?

Despite the threat of two fugitives fugitiving somewhere in the vicinity, we were one of the very last stalls to pack up as usual. I don't know how, but it seemed like we were leaving with more junk than we had sold.

While we were strapping the canoe to the roof of

the van, Sandesh said, "I'm very sorry you didn't sell your canoe, Sheila."

She shrugged. "Can't win them all, Sandesh. Now, as you've been so helpful, would you like to stay for your tea at ours tonight?"

Sandesh shook his head solemnly. "I'd love to, but I've got to do my piano practice. I need to do at least three hours a day. I've got an exam at the end of the holidays."

"Three hours a day!" I said. "You must have very strong fingers."

Sandesh held up his hands and inspected them. "I suppose I must have."

"Don't you get bored doing all that plinking and plonking?" I asked.

"I need to do it if I want to get good. That's what Mum says anyway. It's how Mum got to where she is today."

Aunty Sheila glared at me as she said, "That's an excellent attitude, Sandesh," which probably meant my attitude had been less than excellent. "What pieces are you learning?"

"Johann Sebastian Bach, the fourth and sixth

movement from English Suite No.2 in A minor."

I blinked twice. "Not exactly a catchy title, is it?"

"No," Sandesh admitted. "I'm not massively into classical music. But Mum says I need to get through the grade exams first, then I can choose what to play. She doesn't really like me playing other stuff."

"And what other stuff do you like to play, Sandesh?" Aunty Sheila asked.

"Rock or pop pieces, I guess. Current stuff usually, but I'm really into Paul Castellini. I know he's old-school, but his music is just so...happy, you know?"

"Lucy's mum used to *love* Paul Castellini back in the eighties. We went to quite a few of his concerts together."

"Did she love him? Really?" I said, my heart leaping a little as I thought about Mum's photo and my foolproof plan again.

Aunty Sheila opened the door of the van and climbed into the driver's seat. "Did she? She was obsessed! Don't know why though – I always thought he was a bit of a wally. Wore excruciatingly tight leather trousers and didn't like to speak to the *public*. I think he thought not speaking made him seem more special than he was. Could write a catchy song though, I'll give him that."

I wasn't really listening to what Aunty Sheila said after the "wally" comment. I was thinking about only one thing: Mum loved Paul Castellini. Aunty Sheila had said so! He really *was* the thing that was going to make her happy again. I stood there with my hand on the door handle, thinking about how I could bring them back together, until Aunty Sheila shouted, "Lucy, love, it's a handle – you need to pull it to make the door open."

Back at Aunty Sheila's, Sandesh helped carry the canoe back into the sitting room and then watched as I rearranged my mattress, pillow and sleeping bag inside it.

He looked like he wanted to say something, so I got to the point and said, "Sandesh, why are you hovering around my canoe-bed? Do you want to ask me something or are you just hanging around with the hope we might go for a paddle?"

He nodded and shuffled from foot to foot. "Look, Lucy, everyone in Year Six knows you have sick skills at fixing things."

He was right, I did have sick skills, and I knew where he was going with this. "You want to come back tomorrow so I can help fix your new-old phone?"

"Only if you don't mind."

Even though I had my Paul Castellini / Fix Mum plan to put into motion, I realized I didn't mind. I didn't mind at all. I couldn't remember the last time I'd had a friend round. I had *some* friends at school, but I'd never let them come over to my house. You know, in case they started asking too many questions about Mum. Obviously, school knew my situation, but I did my best to hide the full story from my classmates. I still don't know how Billy Griggs found out.

But somehow, suddenly, Sandesh felt different. It was like he understood. Okay, so maybe that was just because he kept saying "I understand" all the time. Who knows? But anyway, whatever it was, I liked having him around.

"Yeah, that would be okay," I said, as coolly as I

could – because he didn't need to know that I was a bit pleased he'd asked.

Sandesh wasn't worried about playing it cool. His smile stretched so far, I wondered if the ends might meet at the back of his head. "That's brilliant! I'm sure my grandparents won't mind me coming round again. Thanks, Lucy. You're the best!"

He'd said I was the best and I realized that mattered to me. I couldn't help myself – I found I was smiling right back at him.

He waved at me the whole way from the sitting room to the back door.

The longest selfie relay chain consisted of 1,007 people in China

The camera I'd been trying to fix was proving to be a total and utter pain in the pliers. By the time Sandesh arrived at the shed the following morning, I had completely lost my temper with it and launched it towards the door with a good deal of savagery. Luckily Sandesh ducked in time, or my response to his, "Isn't it a brilliant morning, Lucy?" would have been a Campian ED10 right in the face. I would have felt fully horrendous if I had accidentally broken *his* nose too.

He placed his phone on the worktop like it was the most precious thing in the universe and then slid a scrap of paper over to me.

"What's this?" I recognized the scrambly blue numbers as his handwriting. Sandesh has really terrible handwriting. It's like he's been holding his pen with his foot. I have rather good handwriting in comparison, but it wasn't the time to point that out.

He nodded at the paper and his brown cheeks flushed. "It's a phone number."

There was a tiny awkward silence where I thought it might be *his* number, but fortunately he explained, "For Paul Castellini. Well, for the company where his agent works."

I think I stared at him with my mouth fully open for several seconds – minutes, maybe.

"Yesterday, I dunno, I kind of sensed that Paul Castellini might be important to you for some reason... For your mum, maybe?"

Those were some pretty freakily spot-on senses he was in possession of. I had NO idea how or if he knew what I was planning, and I had no idea what I should say.

So rather than saying thank you like I should have, I didn't say anything. Instead, I took off my glasses, cleaned them on my jumper and then began unscrewing the back of his phone with my teeny-tiny screwdriver. Sometimes the best way to get through awkward situations is to pretend they aren't happening.

When the back of the phone popped off, I could see there was a pay-as-you-go SIM inside. I put on my most professional engineering voice. "You might get lucky here, Sandesh. There might be some cash left on this."

"Reckon I might already have used up my luck allowance for a while."

"Luck? You only found an old phone at a car boot."

"I meant I'm lucky because my grandparents live next door to your aunty and now we get to hang out with each other."

I DID NOT take my eyes off the back of the phone. Sandesh had turned out to be a serious oversharer. He was so not like that at school. It made me wonder why he'd only ever talked about world records in class. He'd never talked about himself or mentioned anything about his family – like the fact that his mum was apparently some amazing piano player. Then again, maybe he had, and I just hadn't been listening.

I twiddled away for a bit before plucking up the courage to ask him about it. When he started looking through a box of damaged insurance-meerkat dolls Aunty Sheila had mended, I went for it.

"Sandesh, when we were at school, why did you only ever talk about stuff like 'the largest lobster ever found was back in 1977 and it was two-thirds the size of a Dalmatian dog'?"

"You remember that?"

"Who'd forget a lobster-dog? But seriously, why don't you just talk *talk* at school?"

He shrugged at a meerkat and said, "When I arrived in Year Five, I was asked to tell everyone about myself. I said a few things about my old school in London and about my family – I named all my uncles and aunties and then my thirty-two cousins."

I did remember that. Sandesh's talk had gone on a bit. I couldn't believe that one kid could be related to so many other people. I only really had Mum and Aunty Sheila who I could call family.

"I also said how I love playing the piano. That one day I hope to be a pop star, but even if that doesn't happen I'll always play the piano, because music fills me with happiness."

"Right." That probably wouldn't have gone down brilliantly with Billy and his crew.

"And then I explained how I've loved world records since I was a really young kid. That it's so cool that humans are capable of some truly amazing things and, to demonstrate, I told you all about Gareth Sanders, who **ironed non-stop** for one hundred hours."

I definitely remembered that. "Okay, so then what happened?"

"Mr Kitchen smiled and said, 'Thank you for sharing, that was very interesting, Sandesh.' But then, at first break, Billy Griggs and some of his friends told me that I was the most boring boy they had ever met. And that I shouldn't speak unless I have something interesting to say."

"Billy Griggs is a lobster-dog-sized jerk, Sandesh. You shouldn't listen to him."

"I didn't want to be boring. Only interesting. And I decided then that I'd only let the most fascinating and interesting words come out of my mouth. And what could be more interesting than **GUINNESS WORLD RECORDS**?"

I should have told him then that he was more interesting than any world record.

But I didn't.

I plugged the phone into a charger from the box of chargers Aunty Sheila had collected. The screen lit up. I checked the balance.

"It really is your lucky day. You've got ten pounds of credit on here!"

Sandesh's eyebrows shot so far up his forehead, I thought they'd been caught in a tractor beam.

"You really are skilled at fixing things." He pushed the scrap of paper closer to me and nodded. "Go on, you make the first phone call on it. I insist."

It was quite useful that he was insisting, because my own phone was sitting in the school office. I'd forgotten to collect it after the incident with Billy's nose. Aunty Sheila said spending the summer without it could be my punishment. I'd been okay with that –

I had no one to call anyway. Except Mum.

I dialled the number and listened to the ringing tone.

As I took a deep breath, I hoped it was a direct line to my mum's happiness.

CHAPTER 9

The longest telephone conversation happened in Latvia and lasted 54 hours and 4 minutes

I held Sandesh's new-old phone in my hand and listened to a recorded voice giving me instructions. I pressed **option three**. I pressed **option four**. I wasn't sure about the next option so I held the line to wait for assistance, but that ended up with me back at the beginning. So I pressed **option three** again. Then **option four**. I guessed after that and pressed **option one,** then **six**, then **three**, and then I heard a voice. It didn't sound much like I expected Paul Castellini to sound. Mainly because it was a woman.

"How can I help you today?" she asked in a hoity-toity voice.

I put on my most grown-up voice, which sounded like my professional-engineering voice, and said, "I would be most grateful to you, Mrs Madam, if I could speak with a Mr Paul Castellini."

"Mr Castellini doesn't speak to journalists. He doesn't answer questions."

"Oh, I'm not a journalist, but it is definitely of the uppermost importance."

I knew I was being very convincing because Sandesh gave me a thumbs up and the woman said, "May I ask what this is regarding?"

I cleared my throat. "Yes, you absolutely may ask what this is regarding."

I paused and waited for her to ask.

Eventually, she said in a surprisingly chippy voice, "Well, go on then, what is this regarding?"

I remained perfectly polite and grown-up sounding and said, "I would be most grateful if I could speak to Mr Paul Castellini and cordially invite his attendance..." (That was a very good bit I had read on a wedding invitation that was stuck to Aunty Sheila's fridge with a corn-on-the-cob magnet.)

"His attendance to what?"

"To come to our house for his tea."

I was doing most excellently. I grinned at Sandesh. I imagined me, Mum and Paul sharing a lasagne at our round kitchen table. They'd be chatting about the old times and all the fun they'd had. Mum would be so happy, and she'd be laughing and smiling. I felt a smile spread across my own lips at the thought.

And then old hoity-toity voice hung up.

I tried five more times after that, with no luck. It was very frustrating. I was going to try lucky number six when Sandesh's phone started ringing in my hand.

I held it towards him. "You've got a call."

He looked very excited. "Who'd be phoning me? Nobody knows my number."

"Answer it and find out."

"Hello, this is Sandesh Agrawal on my brand-new phone."

Sandesh's face crumpled at the response and he said, "No, I do not know anybody by that name... Yes this is my phone, my brand-new phone..." Then his eyes grew really big. "No, I didn't steal it. I bought it.

73

And no, I don't know who Stan is or where Stan is. Where do *I* live? I can't tell—"

And then luckily the battery went flat and the phone cut out. Sandesh just stood there, staring at the phone in his hand like it was a dead budgie.

"What was that about?" I asked.

"I have no idea. Whoever just called sounded really angsty. He wanted to talk to someone called Stan."

"Stan? Do you know any Stans?"

Sandesh shook his head. "I think this could be Stan's phone."

"No, it's your phone. You bought it fair and square."

"The man sounded very anxious to speak to this Stan guy."

"Look don't worry about it. It's probably a wrong number. And even if your phone did once belong to some guy called Stan, there are no refunds at a car boot – that's the **car boot law,** according to Aunty Sheila."

Sandesh looked a little less horrified and managed a weak smile. "Shall we put it back on charge and try calling Mr Paul Castellini again later?"

I sighed. It had become clear that it was going to be much more difficult to meet Paul Castellini than I had realized.

Sandesh put his hand on my shoulder and said, "Don't be disheartened. You have to work hard for the things you really want in life. Take Becca Swanson."

"Who?" I said, a little warily.

"Becca Swanson only became the world-record holder for **a woman's deadlift,** lifting 305 kilos, through persistence and determination."

"Is that heavy, 305 kilos?"

"You kidding? It's about the same as ten emperor penguins."

"Those are the big ones, aren't they? That's a lot of penguin."

Sandesh said, "Persistence and determination," and held his fist out for a bump.

I thought about that for a moment, then bumped his fist. "I guess if Becca Swanson can lift ten emperor penguins, I can find Paul Castellini."

"We'll find a way to contact Mr Paul Castellini," Sandesh said, "even if we have to go to London and meet him ourselves."

And I said, "Sandesh, you have just given me the most magnificently splendid idea."

CHAPTER 10

The country that consumes the most sugar is Belize, where people consumed 62.6 kg of sugar EACH in 1999! That's a sugar mountain the size of Aunty Sheila!

Sandesh looked more than a bit pleased with himself for inspiring my excellent idea as to how I'd meet Paul Castellini. So while he stood next to me, his chest puffed up like an overly proud pigeon, I turned on Aunty Sheila's laptop and opened up a search page.

"Thanks to you, I know exactly how I am going to make contact with Paul Castellini."

Sandesh grinned and said, "You're welcome." Then his brow furrowed and he said, "How, exactly?"

In my most confident-sounding voice, I said, "I am going to go on his show and break a world record."

Sandesh opened and shut his mouth a couple of

times and his forehead scrumpled up even more, which suggested to me he might have one or two doubts about my plan.

I shrugged and began typing. "Come on, how hard can it really be to get a world record?"

Sandesh looked at me like I'd suddenly turned into a flying giraffe. "Lucy, world records are *extremely* hard to achieve. People spend their lives trying to master their skills. You can't just *get* one."

"What about that guy with the really long nose hair? That can't take all that much hard work."

"Are you suggesting you want to audition for **RECORD SMASHERS** for your really long nose hair?"

I glared at him. "That's not what I'm suggesting at all and you know it."

"Because I'd say your nose hair is only slightly longer than average, definitely not record-breaking standard."

"Hey! I don't have—" I realized Sandesh was laughing at me. "Oh, very funny."

I typed in **RECORD SMASHERS** and clicked on the website.

"Look, it says here you have to apply online and

registration closes in ten days' time! If our registered record attempt is selected, we will be invited to auditions filmed in front of a live studio audience AND Paul Castellini a week after that! They'll choose who is going to attempt their record on the day, and the best audition attempts will even be shown on TV. Ten days has got to be enough time to find a world record I can break."

Sandesh pulled a face. "Ten days really isn't that long, Lucy."

"It's loads of time. All I have to do is find a world record I stand a chance of breaking, get selected, turn up to the auditions, get on the show, nail my performance, manufacture a way to speak to Paul Castellini backstage and get him to come and see my mum so she is happy again." As I said it, I knew it sounded next to impossible and, from the doubt in Sandesh's eyes, I could tell he thought so too.

"Do you really think you can do all that?"

"I have to." I tried my best, but I couldn't stop the desperation creeping into my voice. I couldn't quite look him in the eye as I said, "I need my mum back, Sandesh. I miss her."

Sandesh stared at me very hard, then nodded. "You're right. You can do it. But you're not going to be able to do it on your own."

"Are you offering to help me?"

"Yes, I am. I know a lot about world records – you're going to need my expertise."

"That's true."

"And besides, I've always wanted to meet Paul Castellini. He's a legend and, you never know, he might let me play for him and then sign me up to his record label."

He looked at me with big, hopeful eyes, like he wanted me to say something encouraging.

I didn't quite manage this because I just went, "Errrrrrrrr."

His eyes narrowed. "Errrrr, what, Lucy?"

I did not want to completely dash his hopes, so I said, "Errrrr, yes, Sandesh. You are right, you never know. If someone can grow their nose hair to the length of a horse's mane, I see no reason why you can't secure a record deal with Paul Castellini."

He beamed and said, "That's exactly what I was

thinking!" which seemed highly unlikely but I decided it was best to move on with my plan.

"We should draw up a list of records we think I stand a chance of breaking and then try each one out," I suggested.

"Go on the **GUINNESS WORLD RECORDS** website. We can get some ideas there."

"Excellent idea, Sandesh."

I clicked on a picture of a watermelon. I like watermelon. Maybe a record attempt involving watermelon would be for me.

"**Most watermelons crushed with the head in one minute**," Sandesh read over my shoulder.

I clicked on a video link and we both watched with our mouths open as Muhammad Rashid from Pakistan headbutted forty-nine defenceless watermelons in half, in one minute. I thought I knew what savagery was, but Mr Rashid took it to a whole new level.

Sandesh let out a big puff of air. "What do you think? You want to give it a go?"

I shrugged. "Yeah, why not?"

The shed door swung open and Aunty Sheila

came in, carrying a box which said **PRINCES OX TONGUE, 100 TINS**.

"Hello, Sheila, you're looking very strong today."

"Thank you, Sandesh." She put the box down and sat on it. "What are you up to? Are you two being mischievous in here?"

I minimized the picture of the watermelon massacre. I didn't want her to know what I was planning in case she tried to stop me. She'd only tell me it would end in some catastrophic disaster. I decided to distract her. "Nothing – sorry, but what do you need a hundred ox tongues for?"

She said, "Precautionary provisions," like it was the most obvious thing in the world.

Sandesh said, "I understand."

I don't know if he did understand. I think he just said that to be kind. All I could think about was that somewhere there were a hundred oxes who were completely unable to lick their own lips.

She spotted the Campian ED10 lying on the floor and scooped it up. "Having any luck with this?"

I sighed. "Nope. I don't know why the stupid thing won't work."

She passed it to me and stroked my cheek. "You'll work it out, kiddo. Now the reason I came in is because your mum would love to have a chat with you on the phone tonight."

I felt a little flicker in my heart. "She would?"

"She's really missing you, Lucy."

I swallowed hard. I did not want all my feelings leaking out of my eyes in front of Sandesh, but my voice came out a bit squeaky when I said, "That would be good."

Aunty Sheila tucked a strand of hair behind my ear. "Excellent. Now what are you two going to do for the afternoon? It's a beautiful day outside. It would be a shame to waste it by spending all your time stuck in here."

"Actually, we were thinking of popping to the shops."

"Okay, but don't buy too many sweets. You know, if your blood-sugar levels get too high, your kidneys can't cope, and you end up with sugar in your urine."

"Sugary wee?" It didn't sound too bad, if I'm honest.

She nodded gravely. "Sugary wee."

"There's no need to worry, Sheila. We're not getting sweets. We're going to buy a substantial quantity of fruit."

Aunty Sheila sat up on her ox-tongue throne a little straighter. "Wonderful news, Sandesh. I think you are going to be an excellent influence on my Lucy."

I don't think she would have said that if she had known that Sandesh had agreed to stand by and watch me smash my face into fifty watermelons. Then she put her hand into her pocket, pulled out a crumpled five-pound note and handed it to Sandesh!

"For the fruit, Sandesh."

Sandesh took it, smiled at me triumphantly and said, "Do you hear that, Lucy? I'm an excellent influence."

Because I couldn't decide what I thought about that, I didn't say anything and instead focused on what was really important. And that was getting Mum happy again with my excellent watermelon plan. I had a really good feeling that it was going to work.

But that's the problem with feelings – sometimes, they're not the right ones.

CHAPTER 11

The heaviest watermelon in the world was grown by Christopher Kent in the US and weighed 159 kg (or around 5 emperor penguins)

As I didn't have my bike at Aunty Sheila's, Sandesh gave me a backie all the way down to the Co-op. There was one quite small-looking watermelon left on the shelf. I could not believe it when I went to the checkout to pay and Badminton Bob said it was £3.50! £3.50 for a piece of fruit. We could have bought ten **Sherbet Fountains** and ended up with very sugary wee for that sort of money.

I cradled the watermelon like a baby all the way home. Sandesh started calling it Wilbur and I found myself absent-mindedly stroking its smooth green skin.

I know now that this was a bad move on our parts, because when Sandesh put it on his grandparents' garden wall for me to smash with my head, I found I was having second thoughts.

I looked at Wilbur, then at Sandesh and then back at Wilbur again and said, "I'm not sure I can headbutt Wilbur in two, Sandesh."

"I understand. Do you want to try and break a different record?"

I thought about it for a moment. What if this *was* my thing? What if I was a natural at watermelon-smashing? I wouldn't know if I didn't try. I was doing it for Mum.

I stroked Wilbur's dark green skin one last time. "I'm sorry, but this is something I have to do. I hope you understand, Wilbur."

Wilbur didn't answer, but I thought he most probably understood where I was coming from. I handed Sandesh my glasses and took a step back.

I positioned my head over Wilbur and raised myself up on my tiptoes like I had seen Mr Rashid do in the video clip. Then I launched my face at Wilbur.

Wilbur was not like all the other watermelons. Wilbur

was different. Wilbur was harder. Much harder. Because when I headbutted him, he pinged off the wall and flew straight into Sandesh's arms, quite unharmed.

I, however, couldn't stop myself bashing into the wall and ended up with a bruise on my forehead and a humongous headache.

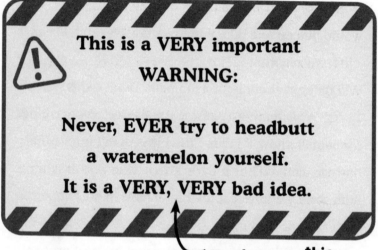

This is a VERY important WARNING:

Never, EVER try to headbutt a watermelon yourself. It is a VERY, VERY bad idea.

Trust me on this.

Sandesh helped me and Wilbur back to Aunty Sheila's so I could go and get an ice pack. She was sieving something that looked like frogspawn into Tupperware boxes, but when she saw me she sprang into action. I think she secretly quite enjoys a minor medical emergency.

"Lucy, what have you done to yourself?!" She pulled out a kitchen stool for me to sit on and gave me a bag of frozen edamame beans to press on my forehead.

I think because I was feeling a bit drifty in my brain, I told her the truth. "I headbutted Sandesh's grandparents' wall."

She slapped her hand to her own forehead. "Why would you go and do a thing like that?"

"I wasn't aiming for the wall, I was aiming for Wilbur."

"Oh my goodness." Aunty Sheila pulled a stool out for herself and sat down. "I thought punching that Billy boy was a one-off, but now, trying to headbutt another... it must be the stress of your mum—"

"Wilbur's not a boy, Aunty Sheila." I was opening and shutting each eye in turn at this point, because I couldn't work out if the bright splodges that were floating in front of me were real or not.

She directed her next question to Sandesh. I think she thought, what with all my blinking, that I might be a bit out of it. "What does she mean, *not a boy*?"

"Lucy's telling the truth – Wilbur isn't a boy."

"Well, what is he then?"

"Wilbur is a watermelon," he said, holding Wilbur aloft.

She did a double take. "Did you hit your head too, Sandesh?"

"Not today, I didn't."

"Lucy, please tell me, why on earth did you try and headbutt a watermelon?"

Even in my slightly floaty state I knew it wasn't a good idea to tell her what I was up to, so I said, "It was a game."

"A very, very silly game. What's wrong with hopscotch, for heaven's sake?!" She held out her hands to Sandesh. "Give it here. I'm confiscating Wilb— I mean, the watermelon."

Sandesh was a little bit reluctant to let him go, but we all knew Aunty Sheila meant business, so he handed Wilbur over.

She stuck Wilbur under her arm and said, "I think it's best if we don't mention the watermelon when we phone your mum later."

"Yes, we probably shouldn't tell her," I said quietly.

Even though I was used to keeping the bad parts of my day secret, sometimes it still hurt that I couldn't share things with her.

Aunty Sheila must have noticed something in my voice because she said, "Hey, no glum face. Your mum can't wait to speak to you."

I nodded because I wanted to speak to her too, even if I didn't know what I should say.

Aunty Sheila invited Sandesh and his grandparents to come over for their tea that evening so we could all get to know each other better. I was pleased about this, because I thought they'd be a good distraction from the jumbly emotions that were bouncing around in my brain about phoning Mum afterwards. I was desperate to speak to her but also anxious about it at the same time. What if it was awkward, or what if she was still too sad or tired to speak? Or what if we didn't have anything to say to each other?

Sandesh's dadi – that's what Sandesh called his grandma – was very complimentary about Aunty

Sheila's pumpkin risotto, even though it looked and tasted like baby food. She was a tiny woman – not much taller than me. She had a very wrinkly but kind-looking face and every time she spoke to me she touched the back of my hand. I liked her immediately. She was very happy because one of Sandesh's cousins was going to get married soon, which meant the whole Agrawal family would be together. It sounded wonderful and I couldn't help feeling a bit jealous, even though I know being jealous is not a good thing.

Sandesh called his grandad "Dada". He was wearing a very colourful tie underneath a grey V-neck jumper and had a big gold ring on his finger. After we had finished our risotto, Dada got out a pack of cards and thrust it under my nose.

"Pick a card, any card."

Sandesh's dadi shook her head in dismay. "Oh, not now, my love."

Sandesh rolled his eyes and smiled. "He's learning to be a magician."

"Well, that's just wonderful," Aunty Sheila said. "I love magicians."

I don't think that Sandesh's dada could have been learning for that long, because after six goes he still hadn't guessed my card. But then Sandesh's dadi found it on the floor and said, "Is this your card, Lucy?" so I think maybe she was the magic one.

Aunty Sheila offered us a choice of two puddings – fruit salad or more of her fizzy yoghurt. Except she didn't call it fizzy yoghurt, she just called it yoghurt, like it was your regular non-bubbly type.

Because Sandesh and I both feared for Wilbur's life, we shouted out, "Yoghurt!" so loudly and quickly that Aunty Sheila must have thought we loved the stuff and she gave everyone massive bowlfuls. I did feel a bit sorry for Sandesh's grandparents, but we didn't really have a choice.

Later, we left Aunty Sheila pulling a never-ending handkerchief out of Dada's pocket and went to the shed so Sandesh could pick up his phone. After he had turned it on, he showed me he had fifteen missed calls from the same number. There was only one text message. It said:

Stan, drop made. D.

I told Sandesh to pay no notice and deleted it for him.

Once the Agrawals had gone back home, carrying a Tupperware of leftover pumpkin risotto they probably didn't want, Aunty Sheila said it was a good time to phone Mum. My tummy did a little wobble and I suddenly felt very guilty that I'd been having such a nice time with Sandesh's family when she was stuck in a hospital somewhere, feeling so unhappy. I watched Aunty Sheila call a number on her mobile and took a deep breath to try and make my jumbly emotions stop being so jumbly.

She was my mum. It shouldn't feel so hard. But it did.

I suppose when you really love someone, and you can't be with them, your feelings have a way of twisting about so you can't really look at them clearly.

CHAPTER 12

The most items washed up in 8 hours is 2,250 by Louise Dooey in the UK

I'd been wanting to speak to Mum ever since Aunty Sheila had dropped her off at the special hospital the week before, but when Aunty Sheila handed me her mobile, I suddenly felt really scared. Aunty Sheila must have noticed something was up, because she kissed the tip of my nose and said, "It's fine, kiddo. She's desperate to talk to you."

To start with I didn't say anything, I just listened to Mum's breathing and tried to work out if it sounded sad. I guess she realized I was there, because she said, "Lucy, poppet, is that you? I can hear you breathing."

"Hi, Mum, how are you doing? Are you better yet?"

I felt a surge of something strong sweep through me and it made my voice wobble.

"I'm getting there, Lucy. I'm trying, I really am. I'm so sorry, honey. You deserve so much better than me."

I hated it when Mum said that. I didn't want better than her. I just wanted her to feel better.

Neither of us said anything for a little bit. I was pretty certain I could hear her crying. And then she did a couple of big sniffs and, in a voice she was trying to make sound normal, said, "Your Aunty Sheila looking after you well?"

I looked over at Aunty Sheila, who was washing up the dishes Sandesh and I had already cleaned after tea and pretending not to listen.

"Yeah, she's looking after me well." I lowered my voice. "Although she's started making her own yoghurt."

I think Mum tried a little laugh when I said that. "She says you've been hanging out with a new friend. That's good – that you've got a friend, I mean. Someone to talk to."

"I guess." I don't know why, but I didn't want to talk to Mum about Sandesh. I suppose that maybe I thought if she wanted to know about my life, she'd have to get herself better.

"Do you talk to him, Lucy? I know you don't like sharing, but it's important to talk over your problems and worries with people or they can get too big."

"I suppose." I knew I was shutting down on her, but I didn't think she was in a position to be telling me how to deal with problems. I dealt with problems by fixing them. She dealt with them by getting into bed.

I felt bad for getting cross though because the next thing she said was, "Oh, Lucy, I just love you so much, you know? Tell me you know that."

"I do, Mum."

"I just get so tired, that's all. So very tired."

"I know, Mum, but I can help you get better, I promise you. I really can."

"Lucy, I'm not your responsibility. You should be having fun and being a kid, not worrying about me. It's better for you to stay where you are, just for a little while longer, okay? I'm in the best place for now, thanks to Aunty Sheila."

I had to swallow really hard and take a big breath

before I was able to say okay back.

"And very soon, you'll be able to come in for a visit. Evelyn – the lady looking after me – would like you to come in for a family therapy session."

"Okay," I said, although I'd been to some of those before and though they had helped at the time, it hadn't really made a difference to Mum in the long run. But I'd give anything a go, for Mum.

"Darling, it's so wonderful to hear your voice and to know you're alright. You are alright, aren't you, Lucy?"

"Mum, I'm fine. I promise. Really I am."

"Okay, love, well...I'd better go. Love you."

"Speak soon?"

"Yes, darling, speak soon."

"Bye, Mum, I love you."

Aunty Sheila must definitely have been ear-waggling on our conversation, because as soon as I said that she whipped the phone out of my hand and disappeared with it into the sitting room. I sat down on a kitchen stool and took Wilbur out of the fruit bowl and hugged him. Mum was definitely still sad.

I rested my cheek on top of him and said, "I've got

to find something I can do, Wilbur. I have to. I must be able to break one world record so I can meet Paul Castellini and get him and Mum back in contact. When she meets him, he'll make her happy and she'll get better, I'm sure of it."

Wilbur didn't answer but Aunty Sheila walked back into the kitchen and said, "Lucy, I think we need to have a talk about your slightly odd relationship with that watermelon."

CHAPTER 13

The highest wall-assisted backflip is 3.7 m, achieved by Li Xingnan in China

Considering the watermelon record hadn't exactly been a triumph, I knew I had to move onto something else quickly.

I told Sandesh that he had to report straight to the shed after his piano practice on Tuesday morning so we could hit the internet again. I tried to get him to come before, but he said, "I need to be dedicated if I stand any chance of convincing Paul Castellini to sign me to his record label." Which was a bit annoying, as I thought he should be more dedicated to finding me a record to smash than pursuing the idea that he might become a pop star.

Aunty Sheila was doing a deep-clean of the house, which she likes to do on a monthly basis. While Sandesh and I were doing more world-record research, she popped in to tell us not to use the loo because there was bleach on the toilet seat. I was pleased about this – the telling, not the bleaching – because last time she forgot to mention it and I ended with a red burn ring around my bum.

As another site loaded up, I began to think maybe my plan wasn't such a good one after all. I turned to Sandesh and said, "There must be *something* I can do, don't you think? Something that will get Paul Castellini to notice me so I can ask him to make Mum happy again."

He looked me straight in the eyes and said without hesitation, "I'm certain of it, Lucy." And that made me feel a bit better.

I clicked on a picture of a girl in a lilac leotard all covered in diamantés and read the caption underneath.

"Most balloons burst with the back?" I frowned at Sandesh. "How do you pop a balloon with your back?"

"Maybe against a wall?"

"I'm not doing anything that involves a wall."

I clicked on the video and the leotard girl bent herself over backwards in a way that did not look like it would be doing her internal organs any favours whatsoever. She then started popping balloons in the arch of her back like an angry crab.

"Woah! She's flexible," Sandesh said.

As I was the only one in my class who hadn't even mastered a decent forward roll, I said, "I'm not very gymnastically talented, I think we need to move on."

I clicked onto another page and as soon as I saw the next image, I knew – I just *knew* – that it was something I could do.

I pointed at the screen. "What about that? *That* I could definitely do!"

A smile crept across Sandesh's face. "Oh yeah, you're definitely the person to break the record for **the most clothes pegs clipped on a face**."

"How many do I need to attach?"

"It says the record currently stands at 161."

"So, 162 to break it and knock current champion

Garry Turner from Manchester off the top spot? Seems doable."

Sandesh nodded. "Garry Turner's going down."

I leaped to my feet because I was full of motivation, and said, "To the kitchen!"

I had an excellent feeling that I had the right kind of face for clothes pegs.

Aunty Sheila had exactly seventeen clothes pegs stored in an old ice-cream tub under the sink.

"Do you want me to go and get some more from my grandparents?"

"No, let's give these a go first. I think it might be best to build up over time."

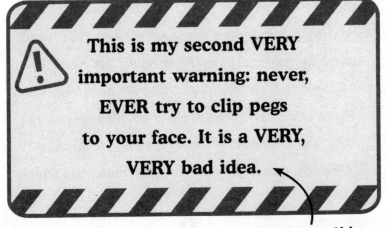

This is my second VERY important warning: never, EVER try to clip pegs to your face. It is a VERY, VERY bad idea.

Trust me on this.

I leaned back against the kitchen worktop and handed Sandesh the box. "I want you to put them on me."

He shook his head. "I'm not sure I can. I don't want to hurt you."

"You're not going to hurt me. I just want you to clip them on. Start on my cheeks."

Sandesh shrugged. "Okay, it's your call."

He slid my glasses off my face and everything went a little bit fuzzy while my eyes adjusted. He put my specs next to Wilbur in the fruit bowl, selected a green peg and held it up in front of me. "You're certain about this?"

"Do it."

He lunged towards me at speed, the peg an angry little crocodile ready to bite. I had a last-minute wobble and tried to dodge out of the way, but he was too quick, and I felt a powerful snap. Right on my left eyelid.

I really had no idea pegs could be so vicious. The current world-record holder had been *smiling* in the photo where he had 161 pegs clamped to his face. I realize now that it is highly probable that he has a very unique type of **super, peg-resistant** skin. A type of skin that I most definitely do not have.

I don't know if it was the shock of something dangling off my eye or if it was really as painful as I remember, but I started screaming at Sandesh. I suddenly felt irrationally angry at him and I wanted him to know about it. "OW! OW!! What did you do that for?"

"Because you told me to!" He was waving his arms about, trying to grab the peg back, but I kept batting his hands away. I did NOT want him anywhere near my face.

To be fair, he was quite apologetic, but I wasn't interested in apologies. I was too busy worrying that I might have a permanently stretched eyelid which would droop over my eye for ever. Like a horrible flesh curtain.

"You said you didn't want to hurt me," I said, quite shriekily. "Get it off! Get it off!"

"If you stop thrashing around for a second, I might be able to."

"You clipped it to my eyelid, Sandesh! That was not what we discussed."

105

Aunty Sheila burst into the room like a human tornado (if a human tornado wore industrial-strength washing-up gloves). She stopped in her tracks when she saw me and shouted, "What are you two doing in here?"

She was also wearing a shiny purple dress with her green scrunchie and she looked like a very concerned aubergine. "Why on earth do you have a peg stuck to your eye, Lucy?"

"Sandesh did it."

Aunty Aubergine turned on Sandesh, who was now cowering against the fridge. "This can't be true! Why would you clip a clothes peg onto Lucy's eyelid? The skin there is very delicate, you know – it could be permanently damaged. **Stretched for ever!**"

I wailed when she said that. Probably because she was confirming my worst fear. Maybe I've got a touch of the catastrophizer about me too.

Sandesh stared down at the lino and looked utterly forlorn. "I...I'm sorry. It just slipped. I shouldn't have done it."

He certainly knew how to deliver a convincing

apology. I sighed and then said, "It's not his fault. I told him to."

Aunty Sheila looked at me with an expression of complete bewilderment. "For goodness' sake, why? *Why* would you want a peg on your eye?"

I wasn't going to tell her the truth, so I said, "I wanted to see what it felt like."

She folded her arms. "And how did that turn out for you?"

"Not brilliantly," I conceded.

"Quite badly, in fact," Sandesh added.

Because my peg-eyelid situation still hadn't been resolved, I said, "Do you think one of you could help me?"

Aunty Sheila snapped it off in, quite frankly, an unnecessarily aggressive manner.

I ran my fingers over my eyelid. "How does it look? Is my eyelid a funny shape now?"

"Lucy, you're fine. But I don't understand why you are doing these ridiculous things to yourself. Perhaps we should do something more normal, like drive down to London and go mudlarking by the Thames."

No one but Aunty Sheila would consider mudlarking normal, and because it definitely wouldn't get me any closer to breaking a world record and helping Mum, I said, "Yeah, maybe," in a way that made it clear I meant, **No, I don't want to wade around in river sludge NOT finding treasure**.

She sighed, then took hold of my hands. "Lucy, will you please stop attacking walls with your face and clipping pegs to yourself? It's dangerous!"

I was being extremely earnest when I said, "I can absolutely promise that," because by then I knew that my world-record attempt would not include either walls or pegs.

"Good, because you have a lovely face, doesn't she, Sandesh? And I don't want you to ruin it."

I could NOT believe she had asked Sandesh if I had a lovely face. What was she thinking? You don't just go around asking people if they think other people have lovely faces, right in front of that person's possibly lovely face. I shot her a look which I hoped suitably conveyed my feelings about what she had said. But she just smiled like nothing had happened. At that moment

I could have quite happily chopped her up and put her in an aubergine parmigiana.

I snatched my glasses from the fruit bowl and dragged Sandesh out of the kitchen before he had a chance to answer. I didn't care what he thought about my face. I only cared about getting my mum well.

I just wanted her home, with me, where she belonged. And if that was going to happen, I was going to have to turn myself into a record smasher, and quick.

CHAPTER 14

The fastest motorized garden shed hit a top speed of 170.788 km/h, driven by Kevin Nicks in the UK

I was still fuming about Aunty Sheila's mortifying face comment when we got to the shed. I was about to launch into a big rant about how Sandesh should literally ignore everything that comes out of Aunty Sheila's mouth, especially if it is about my face, when his phone started ringing again. He quickly flicked it to silent and started chewing his lip.

"Is that same guy still bothering you?" I asked.

He nodded. "I told him again this morning that I didn't know a Stan and that I'd really like it if he stopped ringing me. I said there were no refunds at a car boot and the phone was mine, fair and square. Like you said."

"What did he say to that?"

"He offered me fifty quid for the phone."

"And you turned him down? Why?!"

"I told him that I'd never sell this phone. No matter how much he offered me."

"Why did you go and say a thing like that?"

"You paid for part of it. In my opinion, that makes it a gift. And I'd never sell a gift, especially not one from you."

Obviously, I'm not of the same opinion. People are always selling unwanted gifts at the car boot and I can't see a problem with it. But I couldn't help smiling when he said that. There was something about Sandesh Agrawal that made me lose control of my face.

I rolled my eyes to try and compensate for all the smiling and said, "But still, Sandesh – fifty quid's fifty quid."

He shrugged. "And a gift is a gift."

I looked back at the phone. It wasn't a particularly good one and it wasn't even working when we had bought it. "I wonder why that man wants the phone so badly and who this Stan person is."

"I don't know – there's nothing on it but a bunch of pictures of a roundabout."

I had a look. It was a road-kind-of-roundabout not an at-the-park-kind-of-roundabout. I said, "A road-kind-of-roundabout. Huh. How weird."

Neither of us said anything for a couple of seconds and I tried to come up with an explanation for the roundabout thing. But I couldn't and as Sandesh couldn't either, we didn't think any more about it – because *really*, how interesting *are* photos of a roundabout? And besides, I had more important matters to worry about. Namely, my quest for world-record stardom and a spot of mother-fixing.

I sat down at the laptop and rolled my shoulders a couple of times. "Right, Sandesh, there are a lot of records on this website. We are going to have to be ruthless. I can't try out everything. With nine days until registration closes, there's just not time."

"I agree, we need to be more efficient and say no to things that might be beyond your particular skill-set, if either of us are going to stand a chance of meeting him."

I had no idea what my particular skill-set included, but I nodded anyway and added, "And nothing that will cause me any more physical pain."

And then we got efficient.

It was a **NO** to attempting to be **the first girl to break the sound barrier in free fall**. Basically, because I'm not a professional astronaut and I think I'd need to be one to have any chance. And, speaking honestly, I wasn't even particularly keen on the twenty-five metre black-hole flume at Splish and Splash water park, so a 38,969.4 metre fall to earth from space didn't fill me with enthusiasm.

And it was a **NO** to **trying to spin more than two hundred hula hoops around my body**. I'd tried hula-hooping enough times before to know that it was not something the lower part of my body could get on board with.

And also a **NO** to beating **the world record for running 100 m** because 9.58 seconds is really fast and I only came seventh in the Year Six race on sports day.

It felt like I was making progress; even if I hadn't found my thing, I was narrowing it down. But after a while, our efficiency started to wane. When you look at all the information on world records, it starts to suck you in. There's just so much mind-boggling stuff out there. We'd been looking at the world's **largest display of toothpick sculptures** for a good half an hour before I realized we were wasting time. What was I doing? I needed to focus on my plan to make Mum happy!

"Sandesh, I'm never going to find a world record I can break." I lowered my head onto the table and started banging it in what could probably be viewed as a slightly overdramatic way.

Aunty Sheila walked in at that exact moment and shouted, "LUCY! What did I tell you about damaging your lovely face?"

I stopped banging but kept my head on the table. "You said to stop doing it."

"Honestly, I know this is a difficult time, but you need to channel your emotions into healthy places, not towards my furniture. Or walls. Or fruit."

I still didn't look up, but I said what Sandesh says when he doesn't want to commit to saying anything definite. "I understand."

"I'm popping out for a bit as I have my first baby-goat yoga session at the community centre. Can I trust you not to headbutt anything while I'm gone?"

"Your what?" I wasn't sure I'd heard her correctly.

"It's yoga with goats," she said, matter-of-factly. "Excellent for your well-being."

"Yoga with goats?" Sandesh said, clearly as confused as I was.

"Yes," Aunty Sheila said. "Now can I trust you to behave?"

I nodded, still trying to figure out the goat-yoga thing.

"Good. Sandesh, don't let her do anything stupid," Aunty Sheila said, which seemed a bit hypocritical considering what she was going off to do.

Sandesh didn't exactly agree to not letting me do anything stupid, because he replied, "Have fun with your goats."

Aunty Sheila hesitated in the doorway, then said, "Just behave yourselves."

"We will," Sandesh said.

"I'm talking more to Lucy."

As soon as she had gone, I turned back to the laptop. "Would you say **juggling samurai swords** could be considered stupid? The world record is only four. Five doesn't sound like an awfully big number."

Sandesh zoomed in on a samurai sword. It looked very sharp and pointy. "I'm not sure, can you juggle?"

"Never tried."

"Then probably yes, I would say juggling with five samurai swords could be considered stupid."

"Fair enough." I clicked on a link which said **ODD TALENTS**. "Let's see what else there is."

I scrolled through a few more photos until Sandesh shouted, "Wait! What about that? That looks like something you could do without kebabbing yourself."

"Most tongue to nose touches in one minute." I looked at Sandesh, the glow of the computer illuminating his skin.

I liked the sound of that. There was absolutely no way I could hurt myself by touching the tip of my nose with my tongue. No way whatsoever.

Or that's what I thought.

So I said, "Sandesh, it is brilliant. I am going to be a world-record tongue-to-nose tapper!"

"And I'm finally going to meet my hero!" He nodded at me with a knowing smile. "I think Mr Ashish Peri from India might be about to lose his title."

I scrolled through the details. "Blimey, 142 taps in sixty seconds. That's some pretty rapid-fire tongue-tapping."

He put his hand on my shoulder and said, "I believe in you, Lucy Robertson."

I let him keep it there for maybe half a second, then shrugged it off and said, "Right, let's get record

CHAPTER 15

The longest human tongue measures 10.1 cm from its tip to the middle of the closed top lip and belongs to Nick Stoeberl in the USA

Sandesh used the stopwatch on his new-old phone to time the sixty seconds. I stood up and adopted a wide stance. I reckoned a strong and balanced base would be important. I don't know why.

Sandesh cleared his throat and spoke in a very important-sounding voice. "I'll count you down from four, okay?"

"Yes...no, actually hang on. Four? Who starts a countdown from four?"

"What do you mean?"

"Countdowns absolutely only ever start from three or five or ten even. Never four."

He shook his head. "You're wrong there. When NASA countdown to launch a shuttle, they start at T-minus twenty-seven hours."

I blinked at him twice. "You want to start this count down from **T-minus twenty-seven hours**?"

"Or they start at T-minus nineteen hours, T-minus eleven hours, T-minus six hours, T-minus three hours, T-minus twenty minutes—"

"You know what, Sandesh? Four is fine, we'll go with that."

He grinned at me like he had won the argument – which, looking back, I suppose he had.

He cleared his throat and shouted, "Competitor ready?"

I let out a big puff of air and gave him a thumbs up.

"Four, three, two, one and go!"

I jabbed my tongue out of my mouth and curled it up to reach the end of my nose. Except it didn't reach the end of my nose. It just licked my top lip.

Sandesh's thick eyebrows rammed together. "Stretch, Lucy, stretch." And then he said, "Your tongue is pretty far away from the tip of your nose." Like I didn't already know that.

I brought my tongue back into my mouth, hoping to start again, this time with more force. I thrust it out for a second time, but, again, it didn't hit the target. It wasn't even close. Sandesh tilted his head and looked at me with an expression of what could only be described as pity. But I wasn't going to let him put me off and I wasn't about to give up easily. So on the third attempt I changed tactics and tried to climb my tongue up my philtrum in little steps (the philtrum is the bit between your nose and lip – don't feel bad if you didn't know, I looked it up after). That didn't work either, so I went back to my original plan of jabbing my tongue out of my mouth as hard as I could.

And I think that is when I pulled a muscle.

Well, I pulled my *tongue*, as it is basically all muscle. And I pulled all of it. Each and every bit. My whole entire tongue. And it really, really hurt.

I dropped down onto the sardine crate and cradled my tongue in my hand like it was a slab of luncheon meat and shouted at Sandesh to go and get me an ice pack from the freezer. Except he didn't understand me, because while I thought I shouted, "Quick, get me

some ice from the freezer!" it sounded more like "Quishgemmmeeeesherrrr!" on account of me trying to talk while holding my tongue.

After a fair amount of slobbery shouting, Sandesh eventually managed to work out what I was saying. But because we had no ice, he came back with a mug full of frozen edamame beans, which I tipped onto my poor throbbing tongue.

He stood over me with his hands on his hips and a puzzled look on his face. "I think the problem's that your tongue really isn't that long. In fact, it's surprisingly short."

"Youshinkshhho?"

"And the tip of your nose points upwards ever so slightly."

"Shhhhoooo?"

"It's a question of biomechanics. I don't think the tip of your tongue and the tip of your nose are destined to meet. And definitely not 143 times in one minute."

I have to say, I agreed with him about that.

Mum phoned again that night, even though she was feeling really tired, which Aunty Sheila said showed how much she loves me. We didn't talk for long, which I suppose was a good thing, on account of my injury, but I couldn't help feeling a little disappointed – annoyed, even. She didn't sound any better. Was she even trying? I knew I was. I had a bruise on my forehead and an aching tongue to prove it.

I wanted to tell her that I wanted my mum back. The mum who would do her terrible robot-dancing to the tannoy music when she was buying lipstick in the cosmetics section of John Lewis. Not the mum who couldn't even be bothered to wash her face in the morning. I wanted the mum who hung up fairy lights in my wardrobe when I was little because I was worried there was a monster living in there. Not the mum who forgot to pay the electricity bill, so we got cut off and I had to go to school in dirty clothes, so everybody found out and I got put on a "special" list.

I wanted the mum who arranged my sausages, peas and potatoes so they made a smiley face on my plate. Not the mum who told me to help myself to whatever I could find. I wanted the mum who cared about me. The one in the photo. The one with happiness in her eyes, the one who'd pin me down and blow raspberries on my belly, then stroke my face and tell me she loved me.

But I couldn't say all those things, because that might make her even sadder and then I'd never get her back.

That night, after Aunty Sheila had tucked me into my canoe and I had dodged all her questions about why I was talking with a funny accent, I ended up having a little cry.

It was after she'd kissed me on the top of my head and said, "You know what, Lucy? It's lovely having you here."

It was lovely being there. I loved how I always knew how Aunty Sheila was going to be. That I knew what to expect, that there were never any bad surprises – other than maybe a mouthful of fizzing yoghurt.

Aunty Sheila disappeared upstairs and the sadness crept through my body from my toes until it found its way out of my eyes. I told myself maybe it was tiredness or maybe it was because three different parts of my body hurt. Or maybe it was just because I wanted to be with Mum so much. That I just wanted her to be well.

It was probably all those things. But there was something else too. And even though I could never say it out loud, I knew what it was.

I was crying because there was this teeny-tiny part of me that was beginning to think maybe it would be easier if I didn't go back to live with Mum. And that teeny-tiny part of me made me hate myself in a very big way.

I had to get Mum better.

I had to get her better so I would want to be with her again.

CHAPTER 16

The most musicians to play the same piano simultaneously is 23 and was achieved in Serbia

Sandesh came over after his piano practice the next day to have his lunch at ours. I think this was a brave move on his part, because the cooking smells that come out of his grandparents' house are way nicer than the smell that is produced by the baked-kale-and-beetroot tart that Aunty Sheila makes. But he said he was pleased to get out. His dada had bent every spoon in the cutlery drawer after practising his magic skills and Sandesh said that his dadi was on the warpath.

"It must be fun though, living with an actual magician?" I said, while he wiped his feet on Aunty Sheila's doormat.

"I don't know if you've noticed, Lucy, but Dada is hardly what I'd call magical. But you're right, it is fun, most of the time." He sighed. "I just wish my mum and dad didn't go away so much."

"Oh," I said, "you miss them?" I felt utterly terrible that the thought hadn't occurred to me before.

He did a little gulp and cleared his throat – I think so that his voice didn't betray him. "Of course I do. But it's fine, you know, whatever."

"No, Sandesh! Not *whatever*. Why didn't you say anything?"

He stuffed his hands in his pockets and looked a bit awkward. "Didn't seem right. I mean, you've got it way harder than me."

"Just because I've got my own problems doesn't mean you shouldn't tell me about yours."

Sandesh paused in the hallway and studied my face like he was looking right into me. "Because that's what you do, is it, Lucy? Share your problems? Because from where I'm standing that's an area you need to work on." His words were blunt, but he said them kindly.

And we both knew he was right.

We didn't say anything else because Aunty Sheila bellowed from the kitchen, "Stop loitering in my hallway, lunch is ready!"

Once Sandesh and I had finished what I suppose can be loosely described as food, we went back to the shed to continue our search for something that I could be good at. I was not going to let a few minor setbacks stop me. If I was going to have any chance of getting on **RECORD SMASHERS**, I needed to register within the next eight days. But I couldn't register without a record to break.

I was about to start trawling through the **GUINNESS WORLD RECORDS** website again when Sandesh cleared his throat and said, "Lucy, I have an idea of how we might be able to get on the show."

I looked up. "I'm all ears."

He shuffled from foot to foot. "Okay, how's this for an idea? I was thinking...perhaps...that maybe..."

"Spit it out, Sandesh."

"That I could be the one to attempt to break a record."

I didn't say anything. I just stared at him.

"I was thinking it doesn't matter who goes on the show. We just need to get you through the front door."

Again, I didn't say anything. But I was thinking that it most certainly *did* matter who went on the show. It had to be me. It was *my* mum who needed fixing and it was *me* who was going to do it.

"What do you think?"

"*You?* What are *you* going to do?" I'll admit it, I said that in a very unkind tone. But I didn't understand why he thought he'd have a better chance of breaking a world record than me.

His face lit up and he said, "I thought I might do something on my piano."

I am a truly terrible person, because I laughed when he said that. "*Your piano?*"

"Think about it. It's a win-win – I break a record and show my all-time hero, Paul Castellini, exactly what I can do and—"

"The people at **RECORD SMASHERS** want exciting records to be broken, Sandesh. They want danger or to be wowed or to be grossed out. Playing the piano is a bit, well..." I hesitated.

Sandesh looked up from the floor and stared me right in the eyes. "Say it."

I hesitated again.

He chewed his lip and then said, "Say it, Lucy – the piano is a bit, well, *what*?"

I sighed. I didn't want to tell him, but he wanted to know. "Boring, Sandesh. The piano is a bit boring."

He looked away but I saw the hurt in his big brown eyes and I immediately felt like I was the worst person to have ever breathed air on this planet. I knew how much his music meant to him. I was no better than Billy Griggs.

Very quietly, and still without looking at me, he said, "I wouldn't want to be boring, Lucy. Only interesting. And you know that. I was stupid to think I could ever impress someone like Paul Castellini."

And then he left.

And I did nothing to stop him.

I just stood there and cried.

I think everything got a bit too much for me at that point, and I must have cried for ages, because I managed to get *waaaay* past the stage of crying where actual tears come out and into the stage of crying where I was really only making loud walrus-y noises. That stage of crying can't last for very long because it is physically exhausting, so eventually I quietened down. I wiped my nose with my sleeve and tried to think about what I should do next, but I was feeling very sorry for myself and, therefore, not very motivated.

I did not feel like trying out any more world records. I did not want to go over and make it up with Sandesh in case he didn't want to see me. Really, I didn't want to do anything, but I knew if I did nothing then my brain would start raging like a tornado and even an apocalypse-proofed-shed and emergency foil sheets can't protect you from your own thoughts.

So instead I spent the afternoon working on my Campian ED10. I did everything I could think of to fix it. I took it completely apart three times. I swapped old parts for slightly-less-old parts. I shook it, rattled it, banged it, pleaded with it, shouted some pretty rude words at it and when that didn't work, I even cried over it – which was a surprise, because I'd thought I was all out of tears. But nothing I did helped. I was beginning to think it was too broken for me to fix. That maybe I just wasn't good enough.

Aunty Sheila came into the shed to find me a snotty, dribbly mess and having a full-on row with a couple of camera parts called T-mount adapters. I had them right in front of my face and I was yelling, "Why can't I fix you?"

She gently took the parts out of my hands and put them on the workbench. "Maybe it's time for you to take a little break?"

I buried my head into her fluffy pink cardigan and sobbed while she stroked my hair. I ended up having *another* proper good cry.

She spoke into the top of my head and said, "The fact that you are shouting at photography equipment and have been caught cuddling watermelons makes me think that you're struggling a little bit at the moment. I want you to know it is perfectly alright to feel all the things that you are feeling. Do you understand?"

I couldn't answer because the sadness was sitting in my throat.

"None of this is your fault. Do you know that?"

But it *was* my fault. Everything. I hadn't been able to stop Mum from feeling sad, and I'd been so horribly cruel to Sandesh that I wouldn't blame him if he never forgave me. He'd only been trying to help. I didn't deserve to have a friend like him.

I had never felt so terrible in my whole life.

CHAPTER 17

The largest parade of fire trucks consisted of 220 vehicles and was achieved in the USA

The next morning Aunty Sheila woke me up with her fortnightly fire drill, but I ignored the wailing alarms and stuffed my head under my pillow. I'd known it would happen at some point as I'd been staying with her for just over a week.

When I hadn't appeared at the fire assembly point by the doggy-doo bin on the green outside her house, she stormed in, turned the alarms off and started shouting. I remained hidden under my pillow. I really wasn't in the mood for fire safety, as I was still majorly sulking about Sandesh. It was like, at some point in the middle of the night, I'd shifted from feeling bad about what I'd said to Sandesh to feeling very sorry for myself. And then somehow I had managed to convince myself it was all Sandesh's fault that I had been mean to him – that he sort of deserved it, for making it about him when it should have been all about me. Sometimes, I don't think I'm a very good person.

"Is there something wrong with your hearing?" Aunty Sheila sounded proper stroppy.

And even though I could hear her fine, I said, "Pardon?"

"I said is there— Oh, I see, being clever. Well, you won't feel very clever when you go up in a house fire!"

"If I burned to death, at least I wouldn't feel so miserable."

"That's a ridiculous thing to say. I imagine burning to death is a thoroughly miserable experience. Now get up immediately and go and register at the fire point."

"I don't want to. Leave me alone."

The canoe leaned to one side as she sat herself down. "Darling, I know it's hard, but your mum—"

For some reason, that really annoyed me, and I yelled, "This isn't about Mum. It's not always about Mum!"

Her face suddenly appeared under my pillow and she pushed her nose into mine. "What is it about then?"

"I don't want to talk about it."

"Lucy, come on, talking helps."

"I told you, I don't want to talk about it."

"What do you want to do then – stay in your bed and sulk?"

"I am NOT sulking."

"If you won't talk to me, you could always talk to Sandesh."

"I definitely don't want to talk to HIM!"

She gasped and her hot breath hit my face. "Is this about *Sandesh*? Have you two fallen out?"

I did not appreciate the weirdly excited tone in her voice.

"No! It's not about Sandesh. It's about me. He's made me feel bad because I didn't want his help. Well, I did want his help but not in the way he wanted to help me. He needs to understand he should be helpful in the way that I want him to be." I knew as I said it that I hadn't exactly made myself sound wonderful, but I didn't care, I was too worked up.

Aunty Sheila pulled the pillow off both our heads and I saw that she was wearing her hi-vis fire-marshal vest. "Oh yeah, doesn't sound like it's about Sandesh at all."

She sounded very **know-it-all-y** when she said that, and it made me feel itchy in my brain.

"You don't understand. It was *his* fault I was mean to him."

She tilted her head to the side and looked at me with this disappointed expression, which was very annoying. "Oh, that poor boy. You were mean to him? You should go round and apologize."

"I don't want to go round and apologize. I want to lie in my bed-canoe and be left on my own." What I really wanted was for him to come round and apologize to me.

Aunty Sheila's eyebrow – the left one – shot up her forehead and both her nostrils flared in what could only be described as a very disapproving manner. This was not the face of support and comfort I had come to expect, so I flared my nostrils right back at her.

"I don't understand why you're on his side. You

137

should be on *my* side. I told you why it was his fault. You should believe me."

"I am always on your side, Lucy. But that sometimes means pointing out to you when you're wrong."

"I am NOT wrong. YOU are wrong. Now leave me alone. Go and make some yoghurt or something." I pulled the sleeping bag back over my head. I felt very hot and cross underneath it, but I didn't want her to look at me any more.

I heard her make a *harrumph* noise. Then the canoe rocked back into position and she marched out of the room.

I could hear Aunty Sheila starting to bang around in the kitchen and I wondered if maybe she was making yoghurt like I'd told her to. That made me feel a bit smug for having won. I was still feeling a bit pleased with myself when she returned from the kitchen.

"Lucy?" she said, and before I could answer she emptied a washing-up bowl full of water over me.

I sprang out from under my sleeping bag and onto my feet. "What did you do that for?" I shout-spluttered at her.

She was very calm in her response. "Three reasons actually. **Number one,** you were a whole hot mess of angry. **Two**, I am a fire marshal. And **three**, because I wanted to."

I gaped at her, water dripping off the end of my nose. "I CANNOT believe you did that."

"Believe it, Lucy."

"What is this, tough love?"

"No, Lucy, this is *love* love. Now go next door and apologize to Sandesh. You know it's the right thing to do. And you'll feel so much better if you do it."

"Fine," I said and did a very dramatic sigh. "But I am absolutely totally angry with you."

She shrugged. "I can handle it."

And I knew, deep down, that she could. Aunty Sheila can handle anything.

CHAPTER 18

The longest ever hug lasted for 24 hours and 33 minutes between Theresa Kerr and Ron O'Neil. Crikey, they must have exceedingly powerful bladders

After I had changed out of my soggy pyjamas and also changed out of my terrible attitude, I went into the kitchen and gave Aunty Sheila a massive hug. I buried my face into her and the Velcro on her hi-vis jacket prickled my cheek, but I didn't mind.

In a very quiet voice I said, "What if he doesn't forgive me?"

She tilted my chin, so I was looking into her eyes. "He'll forgive you."

I grabbed Wilbur as a peace offering and headed next door. There was a police car parked outside

Sandesh's grandparents' house and it made me think twice before I rang the bell. As it turned out, Sandesh opened the door before I could ring, slipping out and closing the door behind him. I could tell by the look on his face that something was wrong. Suddenly, standing on his doorstep holding a watermelon didn't seem like my most brilliant idea.

"Is everything okay?" I asked.

"My grandparents' house was burgled last night—"

"Sandesh, that's awful!"

"We were at my aunty's house, wedding planning, when it happened. Well, I wasn't wedding planning – I was playing computer games with my younger cousin, Ajay."

"Are they okay?"

"To be honest, Dadi seems to be enjoying herself. She'll be on the phone to the whole family this afternoon. My mum and dad were going to come back from America but Dadi said not to, that we're fine, and they'll be home soon for the wedding anyway."

I could tell Sandesh was a bit sad about that so I said, "At least they *are* coming back."

Which I think came out a bit wrong because he said, "*I know*, Lucy."

I should have explained that I didn't mean it like that, that I wasn't making it some sort of competition over me missing my mum more than he missed his parents. But at the time, I felt awkward and stupid and I couldn't find the right words to explain what I really meant.

Why is it that your brain never works fast enough at the moments that count?

So instead of apologizing or explaining, I said, "Did they take much, the burglars?"

"No, that's the weird thing – nothing was taken."

That didn't seem *so* awful, but I knew better than to point it out.

"The police said it looks like someone was trying to find something."

"Find what?" I gasped. "You don't think it's anything to do with that phone, do you?"

He shook his head. "Do you remember those prisoners who escaped – the ones Aunty Sheila told us about at the car boot?"

I had a vague recollection of her mild flap at the thought we might have been murdered amongst the stalls of Totternhoe's car boot.

"The police said they were robbers, that they were in prison for stealing a really valuable painting."

"What's that got to do with your grandparents?"

"The police wondered if the painting might have somehow ended up in their possession."

"Blimey, Sandesh, have your grandparents been handling stolen goods?"

He raised an eyebrow at me. "You've met them, what do you think?"

It seemed unlikely, I supposed. "I guess not. What's happening now?"

"The police are taking statements. At least they're trying to. Dada has been practising a card trick on them for the last half-hour."

"Will you tell your dada and dadi that I'm really sorry about what happened?"

Sandesh nodded and then began to kick at the gravel.

I think neither of us knew what to say for a moment and I started to feel awkward all over again, because

I knew I needed to say something about me being a complete horror to him the day before, but for the second time that day, I couldn't think of the right words to say.

In the end, it was Sandesh who spoke first. "How come you've brought Wilbur?"

"I thought you should have him. You know, if we were not going to hang out any more, I thought he'd be happier with you."

I lumped Wilbur into Sandesh's arms and turned to walk back to Aunty Sheila's with my head bowed and shoulders slumped. I hoped the dramatic gesture might do the trick in showing him I was sorry without me actually having to say it, and maybe get him to tell me he didn't hate me.

I was halfway down the path when *finally* he said, "So that's it? We're not going to hang out any more?"

I swivelled around. "Is that what you want?"

Sandesh shrugged. "No, not really. I like hanging out with you. I have the best time."

He was giving me a chance and I grabbed it with both hands.

"And I like hanging out with you too. Sandesh, I'm so sorry about what I said. The piano isn't boring. Well, it is a bit – I mean, the way *I* play it is. I didn't even get past two lessons. But you're not boring. You are only interesting."

And before I knew it, I'd flung my arms around him and was hugging him!

After about two whole seconds of actual hugging, he took a step back and said, "You, Lucy Robertson, need to calm yourself right down. I think you're squashing Wilbur."

CHAPTER 19

The oldest ever elephant in captivity was Lin Wang, who died aged 86 in Taiwan. The average lifespan of an elephant is 60 years

Because Sandesh's grandparents were going to be busy with the police, he came back to Aunty Sheila's with me and Wilbur. After we had perched Wilbur back in the fruit bowl with a Post-it stuck to him that said Aunty Sheila, DO NOT EAT UNDER ANY CIRCUMSTANCES! we headed to the shed. I was very determined to find the thing that I would be good at, so I could meet Paul Castellini.

Sandesh took control of the laptop and after about five minutes he pointed at the screen and said, "You should try this!"

When I saw what he was pointing at, part of me

wondered if he was trying to make me look stupid because I had been so awful to him. But he gazed at me with his big eyes and I immediately felt awful for thinking badly of him.

I nodded. "Okay, I'll do it." I think maybe if I hadn't been trying to make sure he liked me again, it might have taken me longer to agree.

"Do you think Sheila will have a snorkel and flippers?"

"Bound to."

"And what about the hurdles?"

"Hmmm, not sure. We can always improvise and use some of Aunty Sheila's crates and cardboard boxes."

And that's how it was decided that I should attempt to break the record for **the fastest 100 metre hurdles while wearing swim fins and a diving mask**. It's not exactly up there with the most important life skills to have, but if it got me onto **RECORD SMASHERS**, I was willing to give it my absolute all. And there were only seven days to go.

Aunty Sheila's garden isn't very big because of the

massive shed she had installed in it for when the end of the world comes. I guess she wouldn't have known that one day I'd need space for some unconventional outdoor athletics. So instead of the garden, Sandesh and I set up my hurdle track along the pavement in front of our houses. As it was bin day, we had to move all the wheelie bins out of the way. In hindsight, I probably should have done this before I put my flippers on. But you live and learn.

We measured out twenty metres because we didn't have enough box-hurdles for one hundred metres – we decided we could source more if it looked like I was good at it. Sandesh said we could just multiply my time by five to get an idea of how fast I would manage the full distance and because he – like everyone else in my class – is better at maths than me, I believed him.

"You'll need to cover the distance in under four seconds to have any chance of breaking the record."

I looked down the length of our track and said, "That can't be right."

And he said, "You need to take the snorkel out if you want me to understand you."

Which was a fair-enough comment. I pulled my mask up and removed the tube from my mouth. "I said, there's no way I'm going leap over one crate of sardines, one box of ox tongues and another box of inflatable flamingos all the way down to the drain cover outside number forty-seven in flippers and a snorkel in under four seconds."

Sandesh pulled the mask away from my head, let it spring back onto my face, which luckily for *him*, didn't hurt, and said, "That's a rubbish attitude for a record smasher."

I supposed he was right about that too. I had to at least *believe* it was possible. I set about getting myself in the record-smashing "zone" by doing a bit of high-knees running on the spot, followed by a few lunges and then some squats. I saw Mrs Norris from across the way looking at me through her net curtains.

I shouted, "Watch on, Mrs Norris! You are about to see history in the making!" But I doubt it sounded like that, because of my mouth being full of snorkel.

After I was fully warmed up and raring to go, I gave Sandesh a double thumbs-up. I couldn't be sure, because both my mask and my glasses had got a bit steamed up, but I thought he was smiling a very proud smile at me. Looking back now, I think it may have been more of a smirk, but I did not realize that at the time.

Sandesh stood at the finish line and gave his starting orders – which was a countdown from four. I just let him get on with it this time.

"Four...three...two...one... GO!"

And I was off.

Turns out, running in flippers requires quite a bit of adaptation of your regular running technique. Over the course of the twenty metres I experimented with a few different styles. I began with exceptionally high knees, but that got a bit tiring. So I switched to swinging my legs in sideways semicircles, but I wasn't getting anywhere fast like that. I was going to try longer strides, but by then I'd reached the crate of sardines and my first jump. At the last minute I bottled actually leaping over it and decided to leapfrog it instead. I did NOT think I was going to achieve a clean landing, but I did! And I was up and slapping my feet across the tarmac once more.

At the ox tongues I went for a commando-style roll over the top, which allowed me to maintain my rhythm. Things seemed to be going really rather well. I was feeling surprisingly confident and the end was in sight. I only had a few more metres to go before the flamingos. Because of all the success I was having, I thought I might as well attempt a proper hurdle and finish up in style like a top-class record smasher.

My first leg cleared the flamingos, but the flipper of my trailing leg caught the edge, flipped the box over and, before I knew it, my world went luminous pink and I was upside down with my head in a box of tropical poultry with my own webbed feet bicycling madly above me.

It took Sandesh quite some time to leap into action and help me out. I'd like to think he was shocked into inactivity rather than enjoying the moment.

I pulled my mask up off my face. "How did I do?"

He scratched his head and looked at me like I'd fallen out of a tree. "Well—"

"I was doing okay, wasn't I? I mean except for the end, but I can work on that. Was I fast? It felt fast."

"Er—"

"Maybe not under four seconds but it was my first go at it. With a bit of practice it might be doable, don't you think?" Sandesh had a very troubled look on his face, so I said, "Don't just stand there looking troubled with your troubled-looking face, tell me, what was my time?"

"About twenty seconds."

"That's not far off the eighteen-point-whatever-it-was. I definitely wasted time at the end."

"That was twenty seconds for the twenty metres, not the hundred metres."

I laughed at him when he said that. No way did I take that long. I positively hurtled over those hurdles.

I grinned and nudged him with my shoulder. "Saaaandeshhh, what was my time really? I know you're teasing me."

Sandesh's face changed from troubled-looking to uncomfortable-looking. "I can't be one hundred per cent accurate because I was only counting in elephants, but, yeah, it was twenty-two elephants before you attacked the box of flamingos."

"Are you quite sure? How fast were your elephants? Did you say them really quick like this: oneelephanttwo elephantsthreeelephants? Or the way you were supposed to, like this: one elephant two elephants—"

"I counted in the correct elephant speed."

"Dratballs." That was terribly disappointing information. I flopped back down into the box of flamingos. "I'm staying in here with my new luminous pals and I'm never coming out."

"That's an unacceptable attitude!" He pulled me back out. "Come on, we need to think of something else. There are only seven more days before they close applications."

I threw my arms in the air dramatically. "I know there's only a week left, Sandesh. Why do you have to remind me and stress me out?"

"I didn't say it to stress you out, I said it to motivate you."

"Well, you've stressed me out." I grabbed his shoulders and – in a slightly over-energetic manner – shook him. "What if I'm not good at anything, Sandesh? What if I fail? What if Mum doesn't get to meet Paul Castellini again and is sad for ever? What then, Sandesh? What then?"

Sandesh gulped. "You look a bit scary right now, Lucy."

I let go of his shoulders and took a step back, which was actually much easier to do than stepping forwards. on account of my flippery footwear. "I'm sorry for scaring you. It's just *seven days*... I don't have much time."

"You'd better not waste the time you do have. We'll find something you can do, we just need to keep trying. You're not a quitter, Lucy, you're a fighter – just ask Billy Griggs."

I wasn't sure I was a fighter. But what choice did I have? There was no plan B. No other way. If I was going to get Mum out of the hospital and back home and happy again, I had to keep going.

"You're right, Sandesh," I said and I flippered my way back to the house with as much determination and confidence as I could muster. "Let's hit the **GUINNESS WORLD RECORDS** website. *Again*."

CHAPTER 20

The most stairs descended by a slinky is 30 and was achieved in the UK. That can't be right? Doesn't seem that many. Everyone should try and beat this one

I put the box of flamingos back under the stairs and then we carried the crates of tongues and sardines back into the shed. Aunty Sheila would be most upset if her end-of-the-world provisions went missing.

We were just about to start yet *another* internet search when Sandesh noticed his phone was still plugged into the wall socket. He had one message from a number he didn't recognize. It said:

RING ME. WE NEED TO TALK
ABOUT THE AWP.

Neither of us knew what an **AWP** was, but the computer told us that it was the Arctic animal Welfare Patrol, which was a bit surprising.

Sandesh's nose crinkled up like a slinky. "But I don't know anything about the Arctic animal Welfare Patrol."

I shrugged. "Don't call them back then. It's probably just another wrong number."

"It's suspicious though, don't you think?"

"Not really," I said, probably a bit impatiently. "Do you think we could get back to the task in hand? We really don't have long."

Sandesh put his phone back in his pocket and that was the end of that.

Now I sometimes wonder if I should have thought about the message a bit longer. Or at least questioned it more. But I suppose that's the benefit of hindsight. At the time, my mind was focused on one thing and it wasn't Sandesh's weird phone messages. It was the fact that I only had seven days to break a record that would get me on **RECORD SMASHERS**.

After Sandesh deleted the message, he took charge

of the computer keyboard and I was left watching over his shoulder. Again.

"How about **most around-the-world football tricks in a minute**?"

That would be a very cool record, so I said, "Oooh, how many?"

"Sixty-four to claim the record. How many can you do?"

"Let's move on." If I'm being honest, probably one, maybe two at a push.

"Okay, how about **most toilet seats broken with the head in a minute**? The record is forty-six."

"If I can't smash a watermelon, I don't think I've got the skull integrity to get through a loo seat and certainly not forty-six of them."

"**Greatest distance cycling with no hands**?"

"Go on?"

"75.8 miles."

"Don't think the stage will be big enough for that." I'd had enough of peering over Sandesh's shoulder, so I went and sat down on the workbench on the other side of the shed.

"Are you any good at tightrope walking?"

"Couldn't say. But I'd rather not do anything that could involve certain death if I mess up."

"You're being a bit difficult, Lucy." He grinned, picked up one of the defrosted edamame beans which I'd left in a mug next to the computer after my tongue accident, and pelted it at me.

Before I had time to properly react, I improperly reacted and caught it in my mouth. I immediately started gagging, because my intention had not been to eat a manky edamame bean. While I tried to bring the bean back up and then changed my mind and tried to keep it down, Sandesh watched me with a twisty smile on his face.

Eventually, when I stopped all the near-vomiting, Sandesh said, "That's it. That's it! Lucy, we've found your talent."

I could NOT have been more confused.

He said, "Do that again."

"What again?"

"The edamame bean!"

I began to say, "NO WAY!"

But he whipped another one at me.

And I gulped it down too.

Sandesh stood up, his jaw somewhere near his knees. "How did you do that? That was outstanding!"

That's when I understood. I had found my talent.

I, Lucy Robertson of 43 Farley Drive, am **incredibly awesome** at catching food in my mouth. Who knew? I certainly didn't. But I was actually good at something – something that could possibly help me get my mum better – and it felt kind of awesome!

Sandesh sort of breathed what he said next, on account of him being completely, properly impressed, I think. "I have never seen anything like that in my whole life. You were like a frog catching a fly but without the long tongue. Because you have a slightly shorter than average tongue that doesn't even reach the tip of your nose. So really, you were like some sort of magnificent strangely short-tongued frog, gulping down its dinner in a truly astonishing manner."

I quite enjoyed being called astonishing, although the frog bit not so much.

I looked at him, wide-eyed. "Sandesh, I can't look, please tell me there is some world record to do with catching defrosted edamame beans in your mouth." It was a big ask, I realized. But I had a feeling that we were onto something.

He sat down at the laptop and his fingers whizzed over the keyboard and while I waited anxiously I did two little surprise burps. Probably one for each bean. Suddenly he stopped and turned to look at me, a slight smile flickering on his lips.

"No, nothing for edamame beans."

"Oh, bums."

"But Lucy, that doesn't mean we can't try something similar. How about this: **the greatest distance for a grape thrown and then caught in the mouth** was achieved by Paul Lyday and was..."

He paused and I braced myself for some ridiculous unachievable length, like thirteen-and-a-half-gazillion miles.

But he didn't say thirteen-and-a-half-gazillion miles. He said, "One hundred and eight metres."

Er... Hello.

I raised an eyebrow. "Okay, so that's still *quite* far."

"Lucy, that's really far. You've just flipper-hurdled twenty metres, do you think you could catch a grape from over five times that distance? I don't think I could even throw it that far and I have a pretty good throwing arm."

He had a point. "You know what, Sandesh, I can't believe *anyone* can throw a grape that far."

Sandesh rubbed his chin. "I agree. Hey, look here's a video, let's see."

He clicked on the link and we watched Paul Lyday catch a grape in his mouth from one hundred and eight metres away. It was VERY impressive, but he hadn't been thrown it – his friends had fired the grape from a catapult.

"We could try that?" I suggested.

"It took three people to work that catapult, Lucy. We are sadly lacking in that sort of manpower." Sandesh leaned back, ran his hands through his hair and closed his eyes like he was thinking very hard.

I jumped when he suddenly shouted, "No!"

"No?"

"Forget the catapult, I've got a better idea."

"Go on."

He leaned forward conspiratorially. "We don't need to smash a record."

I pulled a face. "Er, yeah we do. That's kind of the whole point of the show."

A smile spread across Sandesh's face. "No, Lucy. We're going to go one better than that. We are going to *set* a record of our own."

"Ooooooh, I like that! Keep talking!"

"Look here," he pointed at the screen. "There's a separate section for submitting **brand-new never-tried-before records.** Think about it – we come up with something totally unique and fresh. **RECORD SMASHERS** will love it!"

"But what? What are we going to do that is *unique and fresh*?"

Sandesh began typing into the registration form. "Lucy, you are going to be **the person to catch the most grapes in their mouth in one minute from a distance of ten metres**."

I thought about it for a moment. With my froglike

reactions and Sandesh's pretty good throwing arm, it didn't seem completely undoable. "You really think we can?"

"I know we can!"

The way he said that with such confidence got me very excited. Too excited probably – I think I might have momentarily taken leave of my senses, because I dropped into a squat position and started punching the air, shouting, "Look out, **RECORD SMASHERS**, you'd better get yourself prepared, because I –" I looked at Sandesh – "I mean *we* are going to win the title for... drum roll please, Sandesh—"

Sandesh did a drum roll on the worktop for me.

"The greatest number of grapes thrown and then caught in the mouth in one minute from a distance of ten metres."

Sandesh pulled a face. "It's quite a mouthful, isn't it?"

And because I was feeling very much in the world-record smashing zone, I said, "Don't worry, this mouth can handle it."

"And so can this arm!"

He looked at the mug of edamame beans and nodded at me. I got the picture. He picked up a bean and threw it at me. I caught that one too. I held up my hand for a high five and Sandesh held up his fist for a bump and we ended up in a slightly awkward hand situation, but it didn't matter – I knew, just *knew* we were onto a winner. Frankly, if this had been a scene in a movie, there would have been some very motivational and stirring music playing. Probably that "**Eye of the Tiger**" song.

I'd done it. No, *we'd* done it. We'd finally found a way for me to meet Paul Castellini and therefore make Mum happy. All we had to wait for was confirmation from **RECORD SMASHERS** that we were in.

CHAPTER 21

The largest collection of squirrel-related items is 1,103 and belongs to Pavel Gerasimov in Russia. I guess we all have our thing

Luckily we didn't have to wait too long for something to appear from **RECORD SMASHERS**, because an email dropped into my inbox two days after we registered our intent to set a **brand-new never-tried-before and definitely totally unique and fresh world record**. I immediately ran around to the Agrawals' to discuss it with Sandesh.

"We're in," I told him. "Well, almost."

"That's great," Sandesh said, "but what do you mean, *almost*?"

"They want evidence that we can achieve at least ten grape catches in one minute before they'll even call us to the live auditions in Borehamwood."

"Boreham *wood*?"

"It's not an actual wood, Sandesh, it's a place in north London where the studios are. But listen, even if we get there, there's still no guarantee we'll make it onto the stage. They say they reserve the right to turn acts away at any time. But, whatever, we need to send them a video before registration closes in five days."

"We can do ten," Sandesh said firmly. "No question. And we'll definitely make it onto the stage, Lucy. Come on, no one has ever set this world record before, how can they not have us on?"

"You're right, positive attitude and all that," I said, not feeling *terribly* positive.

Sandesh and I then entered a period of intense training. Five days wasn't long and we had to use every second available to get me up to standard. I was confident, though, that with focus and determination, my excellent mouth and Sandesh's impressive arm, we would get the evidence **RECORD SMASHERS** required.

Aunty Sheila, however, put a spanner in the works when she caught us practising. With the way she went on, you would have thought I was trying to catch a grenade in my mouth, not a grape. But she said, "Grapes are a well-known choking hazard, Lucy," and then cut every single one in half!

We cycled to the Co-op to get some more, but annoyingly Badminton Bob told us he was all out of grapes. Sandesh suggested we go to the greengrocer and that turned out to be a great idea because that's where we found the **kumquats**.

I'd never seen a kumquat before – to be honest, I thought kumquat was a type of martial art, maybe a cross between karate and sumo wrestling – but it turned out to be a tropical fruit from the citrus family. They're orange in colour, which made them easier to see in the air, and bigger than grapes, so much safer too. I also thought that as they are a rather less common fruit – I mean, who's even heard of them? – it made my record attempt sound even more exciting. In fact, Sandesh later confirmed when he emailed **RECORD SMASHERS** with the fruit-based change, that NO ONE had ever

set a world record involving a kumquat and they couldn't wait to see our application video! Can you believe it? *And* what's more, I was much better at catching

them, so Aunty Sheila had actually done us a favour.

We didn't only practise with kumquats, because they're not that cheap, and besides, Sandesh thought it was important for me to try a range of smaller missiles to really hone my skills.

So once we had run out of edamame beans, we chanced the sugary wee and bought a bumper pack of Smarties. But when we got back to Aunty Sheila's, she spotted them, allowed us to have five each then mumbled something about juvenile diabetes and confiscated them! So it was back to the Co-op, and, because I fancied something savoury, we bought a packet of peanuts.

I think at this point, to be responsible, I really need to issue another **VERY** important health-and-safety **WARNING**. I need to do this for three reasons.

⚠ NUMBER ONE

Aunty Sheila is right. Throwing things into your mouth is a CHOKING HAZARD.

I'm an EXPERT. You are probably NOT.

DO NOT TRY IT AT HOME.

Got it?

NUMBER TWO

Peanuts, in particular, are EXTREMELY DANGEROUS. They're NOT allowed on aeroplanes, not because they'll cause them to drop out of the sky, but because a lot of people are ALLERGIC to them. You can't go FLINGING peanuts around willy-nilly; we're not even allowed them at school.

NUMBER THREE

(This mainly has to do with park-based training locations):

SQUIZZERS – that's what Mum calls squirrels – may look cute, but they are almost as DANGEROUS as peanuts when motivated.

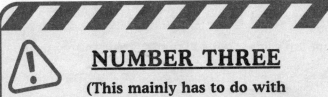

So think about that for a moment, if you will.

Once I'd paid Badminton Bob, I said to Sandesh, "Rather than head back to Aunty Sheila's, why don't we have a change of scenery and practise down at the swings?"

"That's a fantastic idea, Lucy!" he said.

And I thought it was too – but if I'd known what would happen down at the swings, I might not have been so keen.

As I was getting most excellent at catching missiles in my mouth, Sandesh asked if I was ready for some **extreme training**.

I said, "I absolutely am," because that is the attitude a **world-record smasher** needs to have.

Sandesh's idea for **extreme training** basically involved him sitting cross-legged on the roundabout while I swung backwards and forwards on the big swings and he pelted peanuts at me.

He said, "This will add an extra element of uncertainty that our previous practices have not had. You just need to time your swinging and mouth-opening and I have to time my throwing while I spin around."

I thought **extreme training** sounded quite exciting.

The first few attempts, however, were a disaster. If I hadn't been wearing my glasses, I would have got more than one peanut in the eyeball. Actually, I should add a **number four** to my earlier safety warning in respect of eye health and flying food: **if you don't wear glasses, wear goggles or even a scuba mask**.

It was far trickier than either of us had predicted. At the time, I mainly blamed Sandesh for his terrible throws and insisted that I was doing my bit just fine, but really it was me who was the problem. I did that thing where you get cross at someone else because you're angry at yourself, and I shouted at him for his rubbish aim, but it was me who couldn't manage to catch a single flying peanut. I suppose, in the end, I got what I deserved.

While we didn't manage any successful catches, what we did manage to do was scatter peanuts all over the park and lure a very large and overly self-assured squirrel down from his treetop hiding place. (You might be getting an idea here about the importance of number three in my health warnings list.)

The little grey chancer must have been there for

some time, but neither Sandesh nor I noticed because we were focusing so hard on my very important training. Mr Squirrel must have finished all the peanuts from the floor and, rather than being satisfied with his fill, old greedy nutkins wanted more.

I had just made Sandesh swap positions with me so I could show him what I had decided he was doing wrong. I really was in a proper old grump. I was busy demonstrating the "correct" throwing action when it happened.

I didn't see it coming.

Like all good assassins, the squirrel leaped at me from behind and went right for my neck. As the squirrel's teeny claws dug into my skin, I screamed. Understandable. Then I jumped up and scattered peanuts all over myself and the roundabout. The squirrel must have thought all his squirrelly Christmases had come at once because there were peanuts EVERYWHERE. But mainly all over me! I looked to Sandesh for some help but he was swinging backwards and forwards, sort of mesmerized by what was unfolding in front of him. Also understandable.

I always had the impression squizzers were gentle and cuddly. How wrong I was.

I tried to grab the squirrel off my neck, but it must have realized what I was thinking and took refuge down my hoodie. This made me scream even more. Very understandable. I leaped off the roundabout, I think in an attempt to outrun the squirrel or something. But, on account of being very dizzy from all the roundabouting, I ran in a VERY wiggly-waggly diagonal line across the playground. I could hear Sandesh shouting at me to stop, but I think I did three laps before he managed to catch up with me and pull my hoodie off.

The little squizzer dropped to the floor, gave me a look that suggested it thought what had happened was *my* fault and then darted off up a nearby tree.

I stood there for a while, sort of rooted to the spot, trying to process what had just happened.

"Are you okay?" Sandesh asked. He sounded concerned but he also looked like he might be trying very hard not to laugh.

I think I was traumatized by the whole thing because I could barely string a sentence together, but rather than admit that and because I was embarrassed, I said, "Sandesh, yes fine am I you thank. Only was a squirrel! Nuts." Which didn't really make much sense.

Sandesh chuckled a little and said, "You're welcome."

I wasn't sure why I should be welcome, and my face must have said that, because he said, "For saving you."

I was a bit cross and could not see the funny side of needing to be saved from a squirrel, so I didn't respond.

He gave me a gentle nudge with his elbow and said, "Come on, Lucy, you have to admit, saving someone from being clawed by an ill-mannered squirrel is a little heroic. It certainly isn't boring, at least."

Some of the anger drifted out of me and I suddenly felt an overwhelming urge to thank him. To thank him for saving me from a squizzer attack, to thank him for helping me try and fix my mum, to thank him for being my friend – my only real friend. I didn't though, because it's difficult, sometimes, to say what you really want to say.

CHAPTER 22

The fastest marathon in a full-body animal costume was completed in 3 hours and 16 minutes in London by a giraffe named Laurence Morgan

I was still feeling positive that we would get the video evidence **RECORD SMASHERS** wanted. It was the Monday evening during our intense training period and I was lying in my canoe assessing my progress. I realized that the most kumquats I had caught in a minute was five which wasn't *that* impressive. There was some disagreement about the timings because on my best attempt Sandesh hadn't brought the stopwatch and we were back to relying on elephant counting. Also, we couldn't be exactly certain to the millimetre that he was a full ten metres away because we couldn't find a tape measure, which I think Sandesh must have misplaced after the flipper hurdling, so I had to use my thirty-centimetre shatter-resistant ruler from school. So considering all this, I decided it was best to think positively. I was certain that very soon we'd get the video evidence we could send off to **RECORD SMASHERS**. It almost felt like it was my destiny.

Because of all the positivity bubbling through me I was super excited when I spoke to Mum before bedtime. I wasn't going to tell her what I was doing – that was all going to be part of the surprise. I'd found out where her hospital was because I'd seen a leaflet on Aunty Sheila's bedside table. Stamford Retreat – a place dedicated to helping people improve their mental health and well-being.

I had it all planned. Once we'd been on **RECORD SMASHERS**, I'd turn up at Stamford Retreat without telling Mum and say I'd brought someone to see her. She'd probably complain and moan about not having her make-up face on, but she'd still look beautiful. And then, when she found out it was Paul Castellini, she'd stop frowning and her whole body would smile, from the freckles on her nose to the tips of her fingers.

They'd be friends again – just like in that photo.

But when I spoke to Mum that night there was something in the way she spoke, with her voice so small and sad, that made all my positivity bubbles burst. For the first time, I wondered if my plan might not be enough. And then, for the millionth time, I worried that *I* might not be enough. I think she must have sensed that I was getting sad because she said, "Lucy, do you know what made me think of you today?"

I said, "No, what?"

"An orangutan."

It wasn't exactly what I was expecting. "An *orangutan*?"

"I was watching a nature documentary and there was this orangutan on it and it was fixing things with a screwdriver and I thought, *My Lucy is good with a screwdriver*, and it made me smile!"

"An orangutan reminded you of me?"

I heard her laugh. "Yes, it did! Although I suppose you're a little less hairy."

"You suppose?" I laughed. It was good to know she was thinking about me and that she could still tease me.

Then she said, "I'm really trying, Lucy."

And I said, "I know you are, Mum. I'm really trying too."

Somewhat inconveniently, Sandesh had to go away for a few days because he was going back home to see his parents. They had a break in their tour schedule and had flown back to the UK briefly before they headed off again to Germany for a concert. It sounded very glamorous.

As I couldn't practise my kumquat gobbling, and while Aunty Sheila was in the shed sorting through boxes of stuff for the next car boot, I took the opportunity to sort out logistical things for my **RECORD SMASHERS** audition. The first being sourcing some truly awesome costumes to make me and Sandesh stand out from the crowd. And the second being how I was going to manage to give Aunty Sheila the slip for an entire day without her notifying the security services and organizing a nationwide manhunt.

As duping Aunty Sheila was going to require all my brainpower, I decided to look at the outfit situation first. Aunty Sheila had a massive box of fancy-dress costumes that she had collected over the years. To be honest, there's not *all* that much difference between the fancy-dress stuff and what's in her wardrobe, but I wouldn't say that to her face.

When I was littler, I used to love dressing up in all the costumes with her. Sometimes Mum joined in too. I remember this one time when Mum and Aunty Sheila dressed up as this really old pop group called ABBA from either Switzerland or Sweden. Actually, it could even have been Spain. But anyway, they dressed up in these shiny gold outfits and a blonde wig and a brown curly one and they did this totally embarrassing dance routine for me.

When I pulled out the blonde wig Mum had worn, it took me right back to that moment and for a few lovely seconds it made me smile. But then my brain started doing too much thinking, even though I told it not to.

And before I knew it, I wasn't smiling any more. I was crying. Opening up that box had opened up something in me that I didn't want to think about.

I put the wig to one side, did a full-body shake to get the sadness out of me and tried to focus on what I was supposed to be doing. Which was not crying over wigs and sad, absent mums, but finding something suitable for me and my not-so-glamorous assistant to wear.

I decided that the pirate costume was not suitable, and neither was the Oompa-Loompa outfit, even if I would have liked to have seen Sandesh in it. I also rejected a mermaid costume and a nurse's outfit.

I was beginning to think that I wasn't going to find anything, but when I pulled out two matching costumes, I knew I'd struck gold. There was no way we weren't going to turn heads in what I had found. Sandesh might take some convincing, but as he was *my* assistant – whether he realized that or not – I was confident I could get him to do what I wanted. I knew how much he wanted to meet Paul Castellini too. And when you want something enough, you'll do anything to get it.

I stuffed everything back into the trunk. I carefully picked up the blonde wig and gave it a really deep sniff before putting it at the top and closing the lid. Sometimes, it just feels easier to pack the hurt away, even though I know I shouldn't. I suddenly wished Sandesh was there, so I could talk to him.

I put our costumes in a Tesco bag and I hid them right at the bottom of my canoe so Aunty Sheila wouldn't get suspicious as to why I had borrowed two shimmery gold catsuit thingies.

After I had done all that, I found Aunty Sheila in the shed, stacking boxes of powdered milk into a cupboard. She looked very jungle-y because she was wearing a giraffe-print top and these big baggy snake-print trousers.

She gave me one of her big smiles when I walked in and said, "You feeling a bit lost without your playmate?"

"No."

The truth was I *was* missing Sandesh, but there was no way I was going to admit that to her. Aunty Sheila would probably do something embarrassing like tell him or ask him about my lovely face again.

She forced the final box of milk in, leaned against the cupboard door and banged it with her snake-bum until it clicked shut.

"I'm all done here. How about you and I do something together today? Would you like that?"

"Sure."

"Want to fix a few things? We could take a look at that camera of yours."

I shook my head. "Do you mind if we don't?"

I didn't think I could take it if I failed at fixing the camera again.

She wrapped her giraffe arms around me. "Of course, I don't mind. How about we go scavenging at the tip? Might get lucky and find some treasure."

No one would turn down an opportunity to find some treasure so I said, "I would absolutely love to go to the tip with you, Aunty Sheila."

I went and got our protective gloves and goggles and Aunty Sheila went online to check that my tetanus injection was up-to-date.

After I buckled up in the front seat of the van, Aunty Sheila turned on the ignition, then switched it off again and said, "I'm sure your mum will be ready to have you home again soon." She squeezed my knee. "She's getting the best possible help."

I couldn't say that *I* was the best possible help, so I just nodded and thought about how Sandesh and I could get to **RECORD SMASHERS** without raising suspicion.

But my thoughts were quickly distracted, because as we were pulling out of the drive,

I spotted a stocky-looking man standing in Sandesh's grandparents' garden. He was on his tiptoes, peering in through the window, which looked extremely dodgy. I pointed him out to Aunty Sheila. She slammed her foot on the brake and the box of Sylvanian squirrels flew from the back into the front. Just looking at them made me wince, remembering the squirrel attack.

Aunty Sheila wound down her window and shouted, "Oi, sunshine, what are you doing?"

I don't know how, but he didn't seem to notice the giraffe-snake woman with pink hair leaning half out the window of a rusty white van.

She honked the horn and that must have got his attention, because he jumped backwards and almost fell in the flower bed.

"Oi, cotton ears! Is there anything I can help you with?"

The man rearranged his surprised face and flashed Aunty Sheila a wide smile that wasn't really a smile.

"No, thank you. I think I've got the wrong address."

"And I think you'd better clear off before I call the police."

I was enjoying how very formidable Aunty Sheila was being.

He held up his hands. "Honest mistake."

Aunty Sheila waited until he had disappeared down the road. Then she phoned the police and then the Agrawals to let them know someone had been snooping around their house.

"Do you think he might be the person who tried to burgle Sandesh's dada and dadi?" I asked. "Maybe he's come back to have another go and find what he missed last time?"

"I don't know, Lucy," Aunty Sheila said as she turned the key in the ignition. "But I do not like the cut of his jib."

I did not know what a jib was, but I decided immediately that I did not like the cut of his either. There was something very suspicious about that man.

CHAPTER 23

The longest tai chi marathon is 28 hours and 59 minutes and was achieved by Sheila Dickinson (not Aunty Sheila) in the UK

When Sandesh came home, he was very impressed by my hoard of treasure from the tip and he made me promise to take him next time we went scavenging. I said I would, but I couldn't guarantee that he would be lucky enough to find a Kenwood food mixer and a perfectly serviceable foot spa.

I was glad he was back, not only because I had secretly missed him, but because we only had one day left to upload our video, and just over a week to plan our escape to Borehamwood. Which was definitely going to happen because there was no way that I wasn't going to catch ten kumquats in my mouth...

When I asked him how it had gone seeing his parents, he shrugged and said, "You know."

I did not know, so I said, "Nope, tell me."

He did a big sigh. "It was good to see them, and I know I shouldn't complain because—" He stopped and looked away, so I knew he was thinking about my situation.

"But?"

"I wanted to play them the new music I've been working on, but I bottled it."

"Why?"

"Mum, I guess – she's only interested in proper classical pieces."

"Right," I said. I tried to look sympathetic, but I didn't understand why it was upsetting him so much. "You could have just given it a go though, maybe?"

I think he was keen to change the subject, because instead of answering me he suggested we went to the swings so we could practise for the world record and talk through our escape plan. For squirrel-based reasons, I wasn't so keen on that as a location, so we sat on the pavement outside our houses and, between mouthfuls of kumquat, we began to discuss our options. It was a hot day and the paving slabs felt nice and warm on my bum.

Before we even properly got started, Sandesh's phone dinged with a new message.

"Not again," he said, shaking his head at the screen. "I had three others when I was with Mum and Dad."

"What did the texts say? Did you reply?"

"The same as this." He held the phone up so I could see the screen. "And no, I deleted them."

"Time is running out – we need the AWP," I read aloud. "Huh, well they won't be getting the Arctic animal Welfare Patrol from us. Keep ignoring them – whoever it is will get bored soon or realize they've made a mistake."

Sandesh deleted the message. "So what's the plan – how are we going to get to Borehamwood? I can't see a way that won't arouse Sheila's suspicions."

"It's a puzzler," I agreed.

"Perhaps we could tell her the truth. You could tell her you're going to audition for **RECORD SMASHERS**…"

I think the look on my face caused his voice to trail

off. Quite frankly, telling the truth seemed like a terrible idea. Aunty Sheila was always saying how those types of talent programmes exploited people. I don't really know what she meant by that. I can't see how a show that has a massive cash prize or can make you famous could be a bad thing.

"No, this needs to be a completely undercover and thoroughly covert operation," I told him.

"You do understand that there is a chance our audition might make it onto television in front of millions of people?"

"Well, it needs to be completely undercover and thoroughly covert up until that point. Understand?"

"Not really, but I'll do as you say."

"Promise?"

"I promise."

"You, Sandesh Agrawal, are a most excellent assistant."

"Assistant? Since when am I your *assistant*? I'm your co-performer!"

I wasn't going to argue about what we were calling his role when we both knew really, so I jumped up and pulled him to his feet. "And as my most excellent a—co-performer, it is only right that you should have a most excellent costume."

"Costume?" I could tell by the tone of his voice that he was sceptical.

"Yup! Wait till you see what I've found! And I promise you won't look boring. Only interesting. Come on!"

I dragged Sandesh past Aunty Sheila, who was outside in the front garden doing tai chi, which is basically slow-motion dancing with an invisible partner. She'd be flailing around like that for ages, so I knew it was safe for us to try on the gold Lycra outfits in her bedroom. Aunty Sheila doesn't have a full-length mirror because she says it's not healthy to spend too much time looking at yourself. But if you stand on her bed and tilt the mirror on her chest of drawers at the right angle, you can see most of your body.

I'd known the shiny catsuit-type things were going to be a hard sell, but I had not imagined Sandesh was going to be quite so difficult. To start with, he outright refused to put it on, which really wasn't the attitude I was after. I begged, I pleaded, I flattered, but he was having none of it. It was clear that playing fair wasn't going to get him to do what I wanted, so eventually – and I do feel a bit bad about this – I resorted to emotional blackmail and told him that my mum's happiness depended on it. That if we didn't have the right look, they wouldn't put us on the show and then I'd never get to meet Paul Castellini and neither would Mum and neither would *he*. Therefore, the spangly gold outfit was essential.

He looked at me hard for a few seconds, then threw his arms in the air in frustration and said, "Fine!" He grabbed the shiny gold catsuit out of my hand and disappeared into the loo to get changed. By the time he returned, I had changed into mine too.

I can't say he looked exactly joyous about the clothing situation. I knew I would have to keep up the flattery, so I said, "You look excellent!"

"I don't look *excellent*, Lucy! I look like the golden snitch from *Harry Potter*." He started to flap his arms up and down and that made me laugh. I climbed onto the bed and squatted down to try and get a good view of myself.

I looked like a Werther's Original toffee.

It was perfection.

Aunty Sheila must have got bored with all the flailing about with her invisible dance partner, because she was suddenly poking her head around the door and gawping at us.

"What are you two up to? What are you doing in those?"

I didn't know what to say, but Sandesh came to the rescue. "We're just experimenting with outfits and expressing ourselves, Aunty Sheila."

Well, Aunty Sheila positively beamed at that. "Expressing yourselves! That's wonderful to hear, Sandesh. Lucy can be so serious sometimes. It's good for her to explore her creative side."

"It is, Aunty Sheila."

"I knew you'd be a positive influence on her."

And then he positively beamed at that. And I just stood there looking like a toffee penny and being talked about.

CHAPTER 24

The most kumquats caught in the mouth in one minute from a distance of ten metres is fourteen, achieved by Lucy Robertson and assisted by Sandesh Agrawal from the UK (unofficial)

It was no good just looking fabulous, I knew I needed to *be* fabulous and actually catch ten kumquats in my mouth to be in with a chance of getting on the **RECORD SMASHERS** stage at the auditions. I suggested we park the problem of how to get to the studio without Aunty Sheila finding out so we could have another attempt at videoing.

Aunty Sheila said she was going to have a bath following her strenuous tai chi session. It hadn't looked that strenuous, but I didn't mention this, because with her out of the way, listening to whale music and soaking in the tub, she wouldn't see what we were up to outside.

Sandesh drew a line with some chalk by the gate outside Aunty Sheila's and then we measured out ten metres with our thirty-centimetre ruler again. That took quite some time because we kept forgetting where we'd got up to. Sandesh actually got a bit snappy with me, saying, "Would you please stop talking? I'm trying to count."

When I said, *"Would you please stop talking? I'm trying to count,"* in my pretend whiney voice, he said, "Buy a tape measure would you?" and gave me such a dark look that I decided it was best to let him get on with it.

Eventually he flipped over the ruler for the final time and drew another line just beyond the drain cover outside number 47.

"Are you ready?" Sandesh asked.

"I am *so* ready!" I rolled my head and did a couple of jumps on the spot to show I really was.

I held my hand out for a fist bump but this time he went for the high five and we ended up in another awkward hand situation. We really needed to get that sorted.

Sandesh took his phone out of his pocket ready to

record the kumquat action. "Do you think it's okay if I delete the photos of the roundabout to make space?" he asked.

"Are you particularly attached to the photos of the roundabout?"

"Well, the flowers are nice, but no, not really."

"Well, I say, it's your phone, do what you like."

"You're right. Now get into position."

I took my place at the line and Sandesh took quite some time to set up his phone in the correct position on the wall so we could video the attempt. When he was ready, he gave me the thumbs up and said, "Good luck, Lucy."

I said, "Good luck, Sandesh," even though the throwing part of our record attempt really wasn't that difficult. Or at least that's what I thought.

Sandesh nodded and carried the brown paper bag of kumquats down to the other chalk line. He got the stopwatch ready, pulled the first kumquat out and held it up so I could see it, then said, "Four, three, two, one..." and threw it at me. In fact, he threw it a long way over my head.

I said, "What *was* that?! How was I supposed to get that? I'm not a giraffe, you know! Honestly, Sandesh, get yourself in the zone!"

He muttered something I couldn't hear but it sounded a bit like, "How about this for in the zone?"

And then, without even bothering to count down, he pelted another one at me. It was completely the wrong height again, but this one didn't fly over my head, it hit me straight in the belly. Unbelievable.

I looked at Sandesh and I swear I saw him smiling. He said, "It's okay, I think I've got it now."

"You'd better hope you've got it, or I'll be advertising for a new assis— I mean, co-performer." It was a risky threat because we *both* knew there was no way I'd be able to convince another person to wear a gold catsuit and throw kumquats at me, but I needed him to understand how important it was for him to be focused.

My warning seemed to do the trick, because he took a little time choosing the next kumquat and gave a very clear countdown.

It was a good height, it was a good speed. I had to take a few steps back to get into the best catching position, but I knew, I just knew I was going to catch it. I spat it out quickly, ready for the next, which I caught too and then the next one. The kumquats came at me like tennis balls from one of those launching machines, but I was on a roll! When the timer went off, I shouted at Sandesh, "How many was that? HOW MANY!"

Sandesh shouted back, "Fourteen, Lucy! You just caught fourteen kumquats in a minute! We're going to **RECORD SMASHERS**!"

It felt AMAZING! There was no way we wouldn't get on the stage now! Paul Castellini was going to be uber-impressed. I was actually going to do it. I was going to do it for Mum! I started running around in circles and punching the

The most guests at a wedding is over 150,000 at the marriage of V. N. Sudhakaran and N. Sathyalakshmi in India

The morning after we uploaded our video to the **RECORD SMASHERS** website, we got another email confirming we had a spot to audition in front of a live studio audience and we were to arrive at the studios for ten o'clock on Thursday morning. It still didn't exactly sound like we were guaranteed a place, but at this point, everything was going so well, I knew in my bones we'd make it through to see the judges. After all, nobody had ever broken a record involving kumquats – I couldn't imagine they'd turn that sort of **world-first** away.

We just had one teensy-weensy problem and that

was how we were going to sneak down to north London without Aunty Sheila going monkey-bananas. Luckily, the answer sort of fell into our shiny gold laps. Well, it fell onto Sandesh's grandparents' doorstep anyway.

On Saturday morning, with five days to go before the auditions, Sandesh burst in through the shed door waving a red-and-gold envelope in the air. I looked up from the bits of camera lying on the workbench in front of me and said, "Everything alright, Sandesh? You're looking particularly joyous this morning."

"Lucy," he panted. "Guess what!"

I could not guess what though, because he kept repeating, "Wedding, wedding. I'm a genius. Wedding! Wedding!"

I said, "What are you going on about, genius?"

He blurted out very quickly, "Lucy, I have something to ask you."

This all seemed like a slightly over-the-top reaction to a fancy envelope, but I guessed he just really liked envelopes. I said, "Go on, what do you want to ask? What's making you so excited?"

Now, I hold him completely and utterly responsible

for the *misunderstandering* that occurred next. I think anyone in my situation would have jumped to the same conclusion, because he suddenly went all serious, cleared his throat and said, "Lucy, I was wondering if you might...I mean, I'd be honoured if...did you want to be my—"

I stopped him there, because for some reason – probably all the wedding chat – my brain had autofilled the next word to be **wife**! Obviously, I know now that my grey matter had performed some major miscalculations, but at the time I full-on panicked, because even though I didn't know how marriage proposals officially go, I guessed flashy red envelopes and feeling honoured might be part of them.

I said – actually, it was more of a yelp... I yelped, "Sandesh, what are you doing?"

And he said, "I'm asking if you want to come to my cousin's wedding with me. Why, what do you think I'm doing?"

"Why would you be honoured?" (I yelped that too.)

"Kids don't usually get to take a friend, but I asked Dadi and Dada and they like you and said they'd ask and my cousin said yes." He quickly passed me the envelope. I opened it up and took out the invitation. All the blood from my entire body rushed to my face as I realized I'd made a monumental mistake.

"Why are you being so weird? What did you think I was asking?"

"NOTHING! I wasn't thinking anything else at all, okay? Jeez, what's your problem, Sandesh?" My tactic at this point was to shout at him to divert attention away from me.

He frowned and his forehead went all crinkly. "I don't understand what's going on with you."

"Nothing's going on with me. I am totally fine and calm, and I absolutely did not think anything that you need to know about, okay?"

I glared at him, he stared at me, and neither of us said anything for many awkward moments. Eventually, I couldn't stand looking at his bewildered face any longer, so I broke the silence and said in a rather snappy way, "So anyway, why is your cousin's wedding making you so *joyous*?" Sometimes I wonder what is wrong with me. I suppose maybe I was annoyed that he was thinking about nice things like family weddings and I was thinking about important things like how to get to the **RECORD SMASHERS** auditions.

But I was wrong about that too.

Because I'd been an idiot and thought he'd been trying to propose and because I was irrationally angry that he had a big family and I didn't, I hadn't realized that he had been thinking about the plan the whole time. My snappy anger quickly disappeared as he proceeded to tell me why the wedding invite was making him so joyous.

Turns out, there were four reasons.

NUMBER ONE: The wedding ran for three days *including* the day of the **RECORD SMASHERS** auditions.

NUMBER TWO: It was being held in Edgware. Edgware is very close to Borehamwood, the location of the **RECORD SMASHERS** live auditions.

NUMBER THREE: Sandesh said I could go with him. (NOT as a date, before you think anything like that.)

NUMBER FOUR: He also said we could bunk off the wedding and head around the corner to the **RECORD SMASHERS** auditions without anybody realizing.

I stopped him when he got to number four. His plan had one obvious flaw. "People will notice if we disappear from a wedding!"

His eyes twinkled and he said, "Have you ever been to an Indian wedding before?"

"Nope."

"Trust me, there's about three hundred people going. No one's going to miss us if we pop out for a few hours."

"Really?"

"Absolutely. The ceremony goes on for literally ages. Once, one of my aunts disappeared to have a baby and was back by the time the evening celebrations began."

Aunty Sheila was delighted that I was going to a Hindu wedding. She started googling immediately and told me about all the cool stuff that would happen – like that the bridesmaids would steal the groom's shoes and make him pay money to get them back, and apparently there'd be coconut-breaking and foot-washing, and the couple would walk around a holy fire. I was kind of sad we might miss all that. I asked Sandesh if he minded and he told me he had been to so many weddings he was fine about skipping it.

His grandparents were going down to Edgware the day before the wedding to a Mehndi party, where the women get their hands painted with this stuff called henna. We managed to persuade them to let Sandesh stay at Aunty Sheila's. She said he could sleep on the camp bed she keeps in the attic – I couldn't believe it!

"Why am I sleeping in a canoe when you have a camp bed?"

She just laughed and said, "Why would you want a camp bed when you can sleep in a canoe?"

I could not find the words to answer that question.

It was decided we would get a taxi down to the wedding venue the next day by ourselves! Aunty Sheila couldn't drive us as she was going to some auction to bid for a job lot of vacuum cleaners. She was a bit hesitant about letting us go on our own in a taxi.

She said, "I'm not sure about this, Lucy. While you're living with me, you're my responsibility. What if you get in some car accident, or worse, there's an earthquake or a tornado that sucks you up and I never see you again?"

We'd watched *The Wizard of Oz* the night before and I think it had put the fear of weather into her.

I told her we'd be fine. That we'd get in the car outside her house and drive straight to the wedding. Nothing could go wrong. She ummed and ahhed and I pleaded and begged. At one point she said she'd drive us, but in the end, a job lot of almost perfect vacuum cleaners called Henry was too much of a pull, and she agreed.

Our plan was to show our faces at the wedding and then head over to Borehamwood to join the queue of hopefuls and pray our act made it onstage in front of the live studio audience but more importantly, in front of Paul Castellini. It seemed perfect. I tried not to get too ahead of myself as there was still a lot to do and I needed to remain calm and keep my focus. But it was difficult not to get a little bit excited. In five days, if everything went as planned, I'd meet Paul Castellini face to face and get him to help fix Mum and she'd be happy again. My whole body had the jittery-tingles. Everything was hanging on this one moment. If this didn't work, I had no other ideas about how to help her. And I really couldn't think about that.

CHAPTER 26

The most kisses received in 30 seconds is 74 by Florian Silbereisen in Germany

On the morning of the wedding and, more importantly, the morning of the **RECORD SMASHERS** auditions, I had a very tense feeling in my body. Like somebody had wound up my belly button too tight. I think now that Sandesh was right when he asked me if I was feeling a bit stressed. But at the time, I snapped at him, "No!" and then demanded that he kiss Wilbur the watermelon for good luck.

I could tell he wasn't that pumped by the idea because he said, "I'm not kissing a slightly browning watermelon."

Because of the extra-tight-feeling stress-filled belly

button, I shouted, "Sandesh Agrawal, Wilbur is not just any watermelon! He's been with us from the start. Kiss him now or everything will turn out to be a complete **DISASTER** and it will be all your fault because you wouldn't kiss Wilbur!" I gave Wilbur a kiss to demonstrate. "See it's not that difficult! So just do it – do it **NOW**!"

I was a bit out of breath when I finished all the shouting and Sandesh had almost backed right out of the kitchen door.

I grabbed Wilbur and stuck him under his nose. "Please, Sandesh, kiss him or it will be a **DISASTER**!"

He looked at me and muttered under his breath, but I heard what he said. He said, "You're more like your Aunty Sheila than you realize." But then, and even though he obviously didn't want to, he kissed Wilbur anyway and I felt my tummy button loosen just a little.

Before we left, Aunty Sheila took about a billion photos of us on her phone because she said we looked so smart – Sandesh in his sherwani and me in my most colourful dress – and that we'd want to remember this moment when we were older. And then she said something really inappropriate about showing them to our grandkids! I mean, the woman is whole new levels of embarrassing.

When Sandesh went for his travel-wee, she cupped my face in her hands and said, "You are beautiful," even though I don't think I am, and then she kissed the top of my head and said, "Your mum is so proud of you, Lucy. We both are."

I didn't need Mum to be proud, I needed her to be happy. I needed her home. And knowing that it was down to me and a punnet of kumquats to make it happen was making my whole body wind up tighter again. So much was riding on this record attempt – I couldn't bring myself to think about what would happen if I messed it up.

The taxi turned up twenty minutes early, but I didn't mind because I just wanted to get on and get to Borehamwood via Edgware. I grabbed my rucksack containing our gold catsuits, the photo of Mum and Paul Castellini, and two punnets of kumquats, and dashed outside. Aunty Sheila called after us, "Sandesh, I'm putting you in charge. Make sure you text when you get there."

"I will," Sandesh said proudly. He was clearly enjoying being put in charge. I wished I hadn't left my phone behind at school, but I suppose, as Aunty Sheila said, that's what you get when you lose your temper so completely.

After we buckled up, Sandesh turned to me and got logistical, which was good as it helped to calm me down a bit.

"We'll ask the driver to wait for fifteen minutes or so while we run into the wedding and I introduce you to a few people and then, when they head for the mandap – that's the gazebo thing where the ceremony takes place – we'll sneak out and get the driver to take us to the studio."

I stared out the window for a bit and tried to tell myself that it was really all going to happen. I had to think positively. I was going to **RECORD SMASHERS**. I was going to audition. I was going to meet Paul Castellini. And together we'd fix Mum and she'd be happy, and everything would be how it was supposed to be. I was going to do it all.

My little internal pep talk seemed to do the trick,

because my nerves twisted into something else – something that felt a bit like anger and a bit like determination, so I'll call it angry determination. I was focused. I was in the zone.

I was also absent-mindedly eating all the kumquats. It was only when Sandesh whacked my hand and said, "Those are part of your act, not part of your breakfast," that I stopped.

I tried to do a couple of long breaths to relax myself, but I can't say if they worked because suddenly something very unrelaxing happened. We weren't yet on the way to London – in fact we'd only got as far as the back of the city swimming baths – when the car pulled into a side road and a man got into the front passenger seat.

Sandesh and I looked at each other. Something felt off. I began to wonder whether getting a taxi on our own had been such a bright idea. Maybe Aunty Sheila was right to be worried.

I leaned forward and said in my most important-sounding voice, which came out way more wobbly than I had hoped, "Excuse me, Mr Driver, sir. But what's going on? We appear to have stopped. Is there a reason we're picking up randoms from the street?"

The man in the passenger seat turned around and I recognized him straight away. It was the same stocky guy who Aunty Sheila and I had seen peeking in through Sandesh's grandparents' living-room window.

His lips stretched into a smile. But it wasn't a very *smiley* smile, if you know what I mean. It was more of a *sneery* smile. He said, "Allow me to introduce myself. My name's Stan and your friend here" – he jabbed his finger at Sandesh when he said that – "has something that belongs to me."

I couldn't say anything because of all the frightening feelings that were flowing through me. I was like an ox without a tongue.

I could tell Sandesh was frightened too. But he demonstrated some surprisingly impeccable manners in the circumstances and said, "Good morning, Mr Stan. It's a pleasure to meet you."

And then he fainted.

And because that seemed like a very good course of action, I fainted too.

CHAPTER 27

World's most complicated roundabout to drive around – The Magic Roundabout in Swindon, UK. Aunty Sheila got stuck on it for almost an hour once

I think having two unconscious kids in their car caused scary Stan and the driver a bit of panic because when I came round they were shouting at each other. The whole atmosphere in the car was super-intense. While the two burly blokes in the front had a full-on row about whose fault it was, I started shaking Sandesh to get him to come round – gently at first. I had to get a little more enthusiastic when he point-blank refused to wake up. After quite a lot of enthusiastic bordering on assertive shaking, he still hadn't opened his eyes, and if I'm honest, I started to lose my patience. It was really rather selfish of him to choose to stay unconscious and leave me to deal with the situation.

Stan leaned into the back and shouted at me, "Tell me, is he alive?"

That worried me. I didn't know fainting could kill you, so I checked his pulse and was about to listen to his breathing when Sandesh bolted upright. We all breathed a sigh of relief when he did that. Well, actually I screamed, because my face was over his and he headbutted me right on the nose.

While he rubbed his forehead and I rubbed my nose, Stan said, "Now, kids, there's no need to be afraid. We don't wanna cause you no harm."

Sandesh said in quite a high-pitched voice, "You don't want to cause us no harm? Does that mean you want to cause us *some* harm?"

Stan went, "Hey? No harm. Like I said, we don't wanna cause you no harm!"

I wanted to point out that there had already been a certain degree of harm caused by the headbutt, but I didn't think it was the right time to be confrontational. Or the time to point out grammatical errors regarding double negatives, like Sandesh was trying to do. What it was the right time to do, however, was escape. I lunged for the door handle, but the driver pressed a button and all the doors locked. It was a truly terrifying sound.

Sandesh looked at me with these big wild eyes. I reckon I was looking at him with big wild eyes too. Which I'm sure is understandable, because it was a very frightening situation. I wondered if everyone in the taxi could hear my heart, as it was drumming so loudly in my ears.

The driver turned around to look at us. It was the first time we'd got a proper good look at him. He had a bald head with a few stray hairs sticking up, but his eyes were surprisingly friendly. He smiled at us – they seemed like an unusually smiley pair of criminals – and said, "There's no need to get silly. We just need that phone of yours, that's all."

Sandesh said, "I don't have a phone. I'm not allowed one." He would have been very convincing if Aunty Sheila hadn't chosen that EXACT time to call. He rummaged around, trying to turn his phone off, but it was too late, we'd all heard it.

Stan held out his hand and said, "Hand it over now."

I nodded at Sandesh. "Go on, give it to him."

Sandesh pulled out the phone and passed it over with very trembly hands.

Stan smiled and said, "There's a good lad. Well done, fella. What did I tell ya, Ian? Told you we'd get it back."

The phone rang again and Stan hung up immediately and turned it to silent, but it kept buzzing away until Stan blocked the number.

Because they had what they wanted, I thought it would be a good time to remind them of the small matter of letting us go. I managed to stammer, "Can we go now, please? It is just that we have a very important thing to be doing today."

Stan said, "Yeah, you can go."

I reached for the door handle again, but the driver, who I now knew was called Ian, held his hand out and said, "Not so fast. Let's just check it's on here before they disappear."

Sandesh gulped. I gulped. And I started to wonder if they had any intention of letting us go. I felt the panic bubbling up through me and I wondered if I might start

223

hyperventilating or crying or both.

It was at this point that Sandesh slipped his hand into mine and whispered, "Don't worry, Lucy. We'll be okay." It was exactly what I needed to hear, although I wasn't quite sure how he thought we would be okay when we were very *not* okay.

Stan handed the phone to Ian and he began to scan through it.

After a minute or so he looked up and said, "What on God's sweet earth am I looking at?"

"Is it me catching fourteen kumquats in my mouth in a minute?" I guessed.

"Fourteen what?"

"Kumquats, they're a member of the citrus family," Sandesh said, helpfully, although Ian didn't seem to think it was that helpful.

He said, "But where's the other stuff? The messages?

The photos of where our mate Dave stashed it? There's nothing else on here."

"Who's Dave? What did he stash?" I asked.

"Pipe down, kid. I'm the one asking the questions." He trained his gaze on us. "Either of you see anything on this phone you shouldn't have? You delete anything?"

I gulped again. It was a very gulpy situation. "We deleted a message about the Arctic animal Welfare Patrol."

Ian's brow crinkled. "You what now?"

"About the AWP," Sandesh added.

"Ah, I see." Ian nodded like he understood. "You see any photos?"

Sandesh said, "Yes we did, but they weren't very interesting."

And I said, "Only boring."

And Stan said, "Why don't you let us be the judge of that? What did you see?"

"We saw a whole bunch of photos of a roundabout."

When Sandesh said that, Ian and Stan looked at each other.

"A road-kind-of-roundabout, not an at-the-park-kind-of-roundabout," I added.

"You think you'd remember that roundabout if you saw it again?"

I shrugged. "I dunno, I doubt it, but maybe?"

Ian whistled. "Now, kids, seems we have a slight situation here."

Frankly, I thought *that* was an understatement.

"What I propose is this: you help us find that roundabout and then we'll let you go."

Sandesh cleared his throat and said, "That is a very kind offer, erm...sir. But we'll probably pass on that...if you don't mind."

Ian cracked his knuckles in a somewhat menacing way and said, "Sorry, son, that's not going to work for us. See, Dave's the only person besides you two who knows where this roundabout is and he's not currently contactable."

"You can't kidnap us!" I shouted. "We're busy!"

A full schedule probably wasn't the most compelling reason as to why we shouldn't be kidnapped, but it seemed to raise a bit of doubt in Stan anyway because he said, "Ian, mate, kidnapping kids wasn't part of the plan. That's a serious stretch if we get caught."

But Ian said, "I don't wanna hear it. Look, we can't go round digging up every single roundabout in Luton. People will get suspicious."

As a suspicious person myself, I wanted to know why they were planning to dig up a roundabout, so rather bravely I said, "Why do you need to dig up a roundabout in Luton?"

Stan said, "Now you've gone and done it, mate. The kid knows we've hidden the painting on a roundabout in Luton!"

Sandesh said, "What painting?"

Ian slapped Stan around the head and said, "Stan, you numpty, they didn't know about the painting, but now look what you've gone and done. You've only gone and told them."

"Ooh," I said. "Is that the painting the escaped prisoners stole? The one the police were looking for?"

I immediately regretted saying that because they both turned to look at me and Ian said, "Well, this is just chuffing marvellous, this. What are we going to do with them now? They know too much."

That worried me, because I've seen enough films where people know stuff they shouldn't and they do not usually get a very happy ending.

"We really don't know anything," I said.

"Nothing at all," Sandesh agreed. "Nothing about a stolen painting *or* a roundabout."

I gave him my best *I can't believe you just said that* look.

Stan said, "I think they *do* know something. What's the plan now, Ian?"

"I don't know, Stan."

"Tricky, tricky, tricky," Ian said, rubbing his face.

The car fell quiet for a while – well, apart from me panic-gulping. Eventually the silence was broken by Sandesh.

"Okay, we'll do it," he said. "We'll help you find your roundabout."

I gave him my best *I can't believe you just said that* look. Again. We couldn't go to Luton, we had to be in Borehamwood!

"But only if you promise," he continued, "to do something for us once we've found it."

Ian said, "What d'ya think, Stan?"

Stan shrugged. "What d'ya think, Ian?"

"Maybe..." Ian rubbed his hand over his head. "But they've seen us now and they can link us to the painting – what 'appens if they squeal?"

Stan looked from Sandesh to me. "You gonna squeal? You gonna remember what we look like?"

I shook my head and, trying not to look at Ian's shiny bald head, said, "I don't think I could remember a single distinguishing feature about you."

"We promise we won't do any squealing. But you need to promise to keep your end of the deal too." Sandesh said that in such a surprisingly confident voice that I had to do a double take. He was trying to negotiate with our captors! I hadn't had him pegged as the high-pressure negotiating sort.

But Sandesh's surprising confidence must have shocked Ian so much that he didn't question him. Instead he said, "Go on. I'm listening."

Sandesh sat up a little straighter. "Good. We'll need you to give us a lift to the **RECORD SMASHERS** auditions in Borehamwood."

Ian's eyes grew as big as his steering wheel and he said, "**RECORD SMASHERS!** I can't wait for that show!"

Which was completely unexpected, but as it turned out, wasn't even the most surprising thing that happened that day!

CHAPTER 28

The largest collection of The Muppets memorabilia consists of 1,841 items owned by Rhett Safranek in the USA. As I said, we all have our thing

I quickly realized TWO important things during our time searching for stolen goods with Stan and Ian. I slowly realized some other things too, but I'll tell you about those later.

The first thing I realized was that what Aunty Sheila said about not judging people without getting to know them was ABSOLUTELY RIGHT. The more time we spent with Stan and Ian, the more we realized that they weren't terrifying criminals. They were super silly, proper prize-winning, first-class, top-of-the-deck idiots. How they ever managed to steal the painting in the first place, I do not know.

The second quick realization was that Stan and Ian were not going to kill us. Which was a relief. When the car doors had locked, I'd truly thought it might happen, but after watching Stan struggle to put his seat belt on and Ian unsuccessfully program the satnav for Luton three times, death by their hands seemed less and less likely. In fact, as we got to know them, we started to see that they were also kind of okay.

After they agreed to take us down to the auditions in exchange for our help in locating the mysterious roundabout where their missing painting was hidden, Ian and Sandesh bonded over the best world records in history (according to Ian and Sandesh).

I didn't have anything to do other than sit there being kidnapped, so I took my opportunity to question Stan, a genuine real-life criminal, on what made him choose his life of crime.

He didn't turn around to look at me, but I heard him do this big, big sigh. "I did it for the money, I s'pose."

If he had been facing me, he would have been hit with one of my most disappointed looks. I don't know what I'd been expecting, but it seemed like a very shallow reason. "Couldn't you have got a proper job like everybody else?"

"We needed money. Lots of it and fast."

"So you turned to stealing?" I shook my head to try and show my full level of disapproval.

"We didn't steal it from a person, just some faceless corporation."

I didn't know what that meant, so I said, "You know, Stan, money absolutely does not buy you happiness."

"No, but it can pay for things you need. Important things."

I couldn't be certain, but I thought he sounded sort of sad when he said that, so I said, "Like what? What did you need so badly that you had to steal a valuable painting for it?"

He didn't answer me then because Ian butted in and said, "Here we are, what do you think, is it this one?"

I looked out the window as we drove around the roundabout.

Ian asked again, "So what you reckon?"

I shrugged. I turned to Sandesh and he shrugged too.

All the shrugging didn't exactly please Ian and he said, "Look, kids, we can't dig up all the roundabouts in Luton. We need you to tell us which one it is. Does this one look *anything* like the one you saw in the photo?"

I dug deep into my memory to try and find the image I'd seen on the phone and, surprisingly, I found it. It was a blurry image, but an image all the same. "No, it's not this one. The one in the photo had flowers on it."

"You sure?" Stan asked.

"Yes, I remember that too now," Sandesh said.

Ian turned around in his seat. "What kind of flowers?"

"Colourful ones," I said helpfully.

"What make?" Stan asked.

"Do flowers have a make?" Sandesh asked.

"I remember now," I said. "There were red, orange, yellow and pink ones and they were in these big planters. They reminded me a bit of flowery Daleks."

"So we're looking for a roundabout covered in big flowery Daleks?" Ian said in a tone which suggested he did not completely believe me.

"Yup, and those zebra signs." It was all coming back to me.

"Zebra signs?" He didn't sound convinced when he said that either.

"Those black-and-white ones."

Sandesh tried to help by saying, "I think Lucy means the chevrons."

But neither Ian nor Stan were any clearer, because they both said at the same time, "Chevrons? What are they?"

So Sandesh told them. "The arrows that point the direction around the roundabout."

"Ah, I see." Ian drummed his fingers on the steering wheel. "This is all good, we're narrowing it down."

"Can you remember which way the arrows were pointing?" Stan asked.

Ian clobbered him around the head and said, "They all go the same way, you muppet."

And then Stan said, "Don't call me a muppet, you muppet!"

And then Sandesh said, "Do you think we could pull over, because all this roundabouting is making me feel a bit sick."

And I realized I was feeling a bit sick too. We had been around the same roundabout about fourteen times, after all.

Ian flicked his tick-tock and we headed off down another road. "If you're sure it's not this one we should head to the next."

Stan sat forward in his seat. "Eyes peeled, everybody, for the flowery Daleks and the zebra signs."

Sandesh checked his watch. "How many roundabouts are there in Luton?"

"One hundred and sixty-three."

My heart sank. We were never going to make it to the auditions for ten o'clock. We were going to be driving around in circles all day. Literally. I couldn't let all our planning and hard work go to waste, not when I was possibly so close to meeting Paul Castellini and persuading him to help fix Mum. There was only one thing for it – I'd have to convince them that we could find the painting after I'd smashed my record. I decided that I had to appeal to their better nature.

"Do you think that perhaps we might be able to do this some other day? It's just that I have to be at the

RECORD SMASHERS auditions – I just *have* to."

Ian shook his head. "I'm sorry, kid, it needs to be now. We're on a tight schedule too."

I felt my breathing getting a bit panicky and I actually stamped my foot when I said, "But this is important, this is about my mum. Finding a stolen painting will have to wait. We can do this tomorrow, I promise."

Stan twisted round and I was surprised to see that his face looked as worried as I felt. He stared me right in the eyes and said, "I'm really sorry but it can't wait, because this is about our mum too. She's in trouble."

CHAPTER 29

The largest garden spade is 12.4 m tall and 2.23 m wide and was made in Texas

I wasn't quite prepared to accept that someone else could have a mum who needed helping as much as mine did, so I said, "What do you mean, this is about *your* mum?"

Stan did another big, big sigh. "Today is the very last day we can pay off the debts she owes on her house. After that, they're going to kick her out."

That didn't sound good. And it knocked me for a moment. I spent a little time trying to work out whose mum was in more trouble, mine or theirs. I had not considered there could be other people out there trying to save their mums.

"Kick her out?" Sandesh said. "Who'll kick her out?"

"Mortgage company, I guess." Ian sighed.

That didn't sound good either, a whole company wanting to kick her out.

"Can't she move in with you?" Sandesh asked.

Ian shook his head. "We live there too. When we're not, you know, busy at Her Majesty's pleasure. Grew up in that house, didn't we?"

I didn't answer that because I didn't think it was an actual question but a rhetorical question. We had learned about those in English with Mrs Hunter. I don't think Sandesh had quite grasped the concept though, because he said, "Did you?"

And then Stan said, "We did, didn't we?"

And Sandesh said, "I don't know, did you?" again.

And because we were running out of time and because we were now going around in conversational circles as well as physical ones and because I couldn't bear the thought of an old lady being dragged out of her home by a whole company of mortgage workers, I said, "It's fine, we'll help you find the roundabout."

Sandesh looked at me with his big brown eyes and mouthed, "Are you sure?"

I nodded and blinked the tears out of my eyes and I mouthed back, "Yes, I am."

Aunty Sheila says that no good deed is left unnoticed. I wasn't so sure about that, because once when I found a bird that had fallen out of its nest, I took it home and Mum and I put it in a shoebox and nursed it back to health. When we let it go, the first thing it did was fly over me and poo on my head. Mum laughed and said it was good luck. But she was wrong about that too, because I'm definitely not lucky.

But when I agreed to stay and help Ian and Stan, I think my good deed *was* noticed. Because the very next roundabout we drove to was covered in the most beautiful flowery Daleks I had ever seen.

I pushed my nose against the window and said, "I don't believe it! This is it! This is the one."

Ian rammed his foot on the brake and Sandesh and I both ended up with our faces squashed into the seats in front while being showered with a load of stuff from the back shelf.

"Well, that there's a spot of good luck, ain't it?" Stan said.

"Dave chose a good location," Ian said, nodding his approval. "Quiet side street. Not too much traffic." He turned off the ignition and went around to the boot of the car. "Champion. Let's get digging!"

He grabbed a couple of hi-vis vests, two yellow hard-hats, two spades and a **MEN AT WORK** sign out of the boot of the car. I was impressed by the forward planning, if I'm honest.

Sandesh and I watched from the car as Stan and Ian dug up the middle of a roundabout near the bookies and the fish-and-chip shop somewhere in Luton. I was genuinely very excited when they pulled a big rectangular package out of the ground and I suddenly found myself clapping. Sandesh must have been excited too, because he gasped and said, "I never thought they'd actually find it. I feel bad – I think I may have underestimated Stan and Ian."

"Don't worry," I said, while I watched Stan and Ian trying to work out how to carry the painting, the spades

and the sign in one go. "I doubt they noticed."

Ian and Stan did two trips back to the car. First, they put the painting between me and Sandesh, and then they flung the rest of the stuff in the boot.

"Pedal to the metal, Ian," Stan said. "We've gotta get these two to Borehamwood."

Sandesh checked his watch and nodded at me. "We've got time. We're going to make it."

Stan took a CD out of the glovebox and put it into the player. "How about some music to get you in the zone, ready for your audition?"

I was going to say, "That would be nice, thank you, Stan," mainly to be polite, but Ian slammed his foot on the accelerator, the tyres screeched and I was thrown back in my seat so hard that the words never made it out of my mouth.

The drive to Borehamwood was one of the most terrifying experiences of my life. Ian was determined to get us to the auditions on time and unsurprisingly – and probably because he was a man of criminal leanings – he paid absolutely no attention to the speed limit. Sandesh and I were thrown around in the back, being bashed by the painting and clinging onto the door handles for dear life.

Under the blare of Paul Castellini's "**Best Of**" album, I could hear whimpering. At first I thought it was Sandesh, but then I realized it couldn't be him because he was *singing* – which seemed inappropriate in the circumstances, but I guess he does *really* like Paul Castellini. The whimpering wasn't Stan or Ian either, which left only one possibility – it was me. I hadn't thought I was the whimpering sort. But anyway, I eventually stopped when we pulled into the car park of the **RECORD SMASHERS** studio, because I knew I had a job to do.

When I saw the size of the queue outside the front doors, however, I felt like whimpering all over again.

CHAPTER 30

The youngest ever TV presenter is Luis Tanner from Australia, who was 5 years and 68 days old when he recorded his first show. It took me until I was 11 years and 79 days old before I was on TV

Stan and Ian decided that the studio car park would be an excellent place for the exchange of stolen goods, as there were so many people about that nobody would notice (or some weird Stan-and-Ian logic like that). And they thought it would make them look less like criminals if they hung around with us until they heard back from "their guy Rod with the money".

There was the small matter that we hadn't turned up at the wedding and everyone might be getting worried, but, at the time, we decided to put that thought to the back of our minds. We didn't realize that twenty minutes after we had headed off in a taxi from Aunty Sheila's, another had arrived to pick us up. Nor did we stop to think about the catastrophic levels of panic Aunty Sheila had experienced when we didn't answer her calls.

Unbeknownst to us, our plan to get to Borehamwood without Aunty Sheila alerting the national security services had failed spectacularly. But we didn't know that at the time. And if we had, we might have suggested to Ian and Stan that they probably didn't want to hang around Borehamwood too long.

But as it was, I knew I had to focus on one thing and one thing only: setting the world record for catching the most kumquats in my mouth in a minute from a distance of ten metres so that we could meet Paul Castellini. I suppose that's actually two things, but you know what I mean.

We joined the back of the queue behind a man carrying five samurai swords that I guessed he was going to juggle, and I was immediately relieved that I hadn't decided to try that record. It looked like we were in for a long wait, but then a TV camera crew appeared and, all of a sudden, we experienced a second bit of good luck.

The lady presenter who was being filmed was wearing a very bright pink suit, matching lipstick and a pair of jazzy yellow boots. She seemed to be VERY excited. About EVERYTHING. She was jumping up and down and cheering and waving and shouting as she made her way along the queue, asking equally excited contestants about their record attempts.

When she saw Sandesh, she stopped and stuck her microphone under his nose and said, "Heeeelllllloooo, I'm Trixie Hawker, what's your name? You're adorable!"

Sandesh positively beamed at being called adorable and he said, "My name is Sandesh Agrawal."

"That's an amaaaaazing name! What are you doing today?"

"I'm here with my friend to set the record for the most number of kumquats caught in the mouth in a minute."

Trixie looked at me and said, "What's your name?"

I waited for her to tell me I was adorable too, but she didn't so I sighed and said, "My name's Lucy Robertson."

"And are you helping out with his...
unusual act today?"

Sandesh grinned when she said that.

I said, rather hotly I suppose,
"I am the unusual act, Sandesh is
helping *me*."

Trixie didn't seem to notice her mistake because she turned back to Sandesh and said, "Are you performing your record for anyone special?"

He said, "Oh yes. We are performing this record for someone massively special. We're here for Lucy's mum. Today's a very important day."

Trixie spun back to me and said, "Is this true? Are you doing this for your mum?"

And I don't know why it happened, but I immediately burst into tears.

Sandesh, Ian and Stan all looked mortified, but Trixie...well, Trixie looked delighted. She turned to a woman who was holding a clipboard and standing next to the cameraman and said, "BINGO! Janet – are you getting this? Sob-story alert. Let's make these two a priority. Couple of kids, Sandesh and Lucy, who is crying over her mum. This is TV gold!" She then looked at us and said, "That's a good thing. People will love you two!"

I wasn't sure it was a *good* thing the way she said it, but I did like the thought of people loving us.

Clipboard-Janet nodded enthusiastically and pretty

much squealed when she said, "Throw in a puppy and we could hit all the emotional hotspots."

Trixie turned back to Sandesh and laughed. "Don't suppose your act involves a puppy too, does it?"

"No, only kumquats."

"Shame, but never mind, we've got enough." She turned to Ian and Stan and said, "Are you their guardians? We need an adult's permission before we can allow them onstage."

I looked at them with my most pleading eyes.

And Stan and Ian said, "Yeah, sure, why not."

"Fantabulous, darlings! Let's get this show on the road!" Trixie stalked off in the direction of the front doors, her high heels clacking on the pavement. We just stood there, wondering what was going on, but then she stopped, turned around and shouted, "*JANET!*" very loudly.

Janet promptly dropped her clipboard, then scrabbled about on the floor as she tried to pick it up.

This didn't seem to please Trixie, because even though she could see what clipboard-Janet was doing, she said, "What are you doing now, Janet?"

Clipboard-Janet said, "I...I...I..."

Trixie did a very dramatic sigh and rolled her eyes. "Just hurry up and get those kids backstage."

Sandesh and I caught each other's eye. Backstage – that sounded promising. At last, we were so, so close to meeting Paul Castellini and getting him to make Mum happy again.

CHAPTER 31

The fastest time to eat a Chocolate Orange...is a record that's not yet been attempted! Which means you can try this one!

I think perhaps it was the suddenness of being put on the spot about Mum that made me lose control of my sadness and end up crying in public. I was mortified, but like all professional **RECORD SMASHERS**, I managed to quickly pull myself together, and as we marched straight by all the other hopefuls in the queue, I'll admit I started to feel a little smug.

We were taken to a green room that was actually painted white and had big grey sofas. Trixie went off to go and get more make-up put on – although I don't know where she was going to put it, her face was already covered in the stuff.

Clipboard-Janet told us to wait and that her researcher would be along in a minute. She said we could help ourselves to anything we wanted. After she had gone, I had to explain to Stan and Ian that she probably didn't mean the huge plasma TV, but the snacks and drinks on the coffee table.

I couldn't eat anything because I was feeling a bit nervy-sick, but I watched with a mixture of awe and horror as Sandesh chomped his way through eight packets of pickled onion Monster Munch. His tongue must have been terribly tingly. Ian and Stan also got deeply involved in the feasting. I have never seen two men demolish a Toblerone so quickly.

The researcher came in just as Ian and Stan were arguing over whether they could fit a whole Chocolate Orange in their mouths. He sat down on the grey couch and patted the seat next to him. "Sandesh, Lucy, my name's Brussel and I'd love to have a quick chat with you guys, if that's okay?" He tilted his head and gave me this small smile that for some reason made me want to punch him in the face.

But I didn't have to because Stan said, "Sorry, mate.

Did you say your name is Brussel?"

"That's right, like Russel but with an added B to remind you I'm B-rilliant."

"Or to remind us you're named after a horrible small cabbage thing?" Ian said, with a very puzzled look on his face.

Brussel ignored the sprout comment – he'd probably heard it before – and turned to me. "So, good news, I've confirmed you've registered with us and we'd love to get you onstage to audition. I just have a few questions for you before that can happen. Now, the lovely Trixie Hawker says you're here today for your mum? Did you want to tell me some more about that?"

I really didn't want to tell him more about that, but I also guessed my chances of meeting Paul Castellini might hinge on me giving him what he wanted.

So I gulped away my worries around speaking about my mum and I said, "I really only want to make my mum happy again."

Brussel stuck out his bottom lip and said, "And why is your mum unhappy, Lucy?"

I didn't answer so he said, "Has there been a

255

bereavement? Or did your parents divorce? Or maybe she lost her job?"

I shook my head and I swear he looked disappointed.

"What is it then? What is she sad about?"

I didn't really know what to say. She seemed to be sad about everything and nothing. Brussel stared at me and nodded at me to go on, and because I didn't know what to say I found myself telling him about how her sadness comes every now and then. And that it makes Mum sort of shut down for a bit. Sometimes not for long, but sometimes...sometimes it almost feels like for ever. I told him about how much I loved her. How much fun she could be and how I just really, *really* wanted her to get better. And to be happy like everybody else.

I didn't look at anybody when I said all that, but when I looked up I could see Brussel seemed to like what I had said because he was smiling. "And you hoped you'd make her happy by performing here today, is that right?"

I didn't need to lie about it not really being about the performance and more about being there to meet Paul Castellini because I decided that was another rhetorical question. And I must have been right about that, because Brussel was already up on his feet like he didn't expect me to answer.

He said, "I'll be back in a minute to take you backstage so you can change and get ready for your act. I'm delighted to tell you that you will be performing today."

Sandesh shouted, "Get in!" very loudly, which made me jump because I'd been concentrating on myself and momentarily sort of forgotten he was involved in the record attempt too. Then he held out his hand for a fist bump and I high-fived it because that was now our thing.

As Brussel walked out the room, he pulled a walkie-talkie from his back pocket and I heard him say, "Okay, I've fast-tracked the kids... The mother has mental health issues. Poor girl. Sounds like depression. Very current anyway."

Mental health issues.

Those words cut through me. I don't know why. Maybe it was hearing someone who didn't even know Mum say it so matter-of-factly like that. People usually softened it. They said things like, *Sorry to hear your mum's having a hard time.* Or, *She just has these feelings she needs to work through. Your mum's just a bit blue, Lucy.* But it was more than that. Mum had an illness. And she needed help to get through it. I wanted to be the person to find the help she needed more than anything.

When I looked up, I realized two things.

One: Sandesh, Stan and Ian were all staring at me.

And two: I was crying. Again. I think all the bottled-up anxiety and fear and worry I'd been storing deep down inside myself was finding its way out of my eyes.

I suddenly felt very small and very exposed. And then I felt very small and very squashed, because all three of them ran over and hugged me. And then I felt a bit better. And then I felt the angry determination again.

Ian said, "You want us to make pulp out of sprout-boy for you?"

I shook my head. I wasn't bothered about him.

I knew what I had to do.

CHAPTER 32

The furthest distance travelled on roller skates while juggling three chainsaws...is another record that's not been attempted. For obvious reasons. Do NOT try this one!

Things happened very fast after that. Brussel burst back into the room and told us we needed to move quickly. He wanted to get us onstage to do our act and then into **"the talent interviews"** afterwards. I rather enjoyed being called **"the talent"**.

We changed into our gold spangly outfits in separate changing rooms. When we emerged, I could tell by the look on Brussel's face that he was impressed by the effort we had gone to.

Stan said, "You look like a couple of shiny pound coins."

And Ian said, "Crikey, need my sunglasses to look at you in those."

Brussel swept us out through the door. "You're going to be straight on after Paul has performed the opening number. He's going to start every show with one of his past hits – he thought it would be a nice touch. Now, have you got everything you need?"

"We're good to go." I patted my rucksack where the remaining kumquats were. I was feeling surprisingly confident, because at that point I did not know about my crippling stage-fright or about Aunty Sheila or about Sandesh's relatives or about the police.

Brussel directed us down a maze of corridors and past rooms full of contestants rehearsing with hula hoops and barbells and juggling balls and roller skates and chainsaws. I saw a man with a Tupperware box full of coloured pegs and said, "Be careful not to clip them on your eyelids because it really, really hurts."

I shot a meaningful glance at Sandesh and he said, "I'm still very sorry about the eyelid-pegging incident." Then he lowered his voice and said, "Even if it wasn't really my fault."

I would have picked him up on that, but it didn't seem like the right time.

Brussel was talking at us the whole time we were walking.

"Will I get a chance to speak to Paul Castellini privately?" I asked as casually as I could – but in all honesty it did come out a little high-pitched.

Sandesh said in a fairly high pitch too, "It would be just so cool if we could speak to Paul Castellini. I'm his biggest-ever fan. Like, the biggest!"

Brussel stopped in his tracks and eyed us in what could only be described as a somewhat suspicious manner. "Listen, you kids aren't going to do anything weird, are you?"

We were about to go onstage in matching shiny gold catsuit things so I could catch kumquats in my mouth, so I didn't quite know how to answer that.

"It is well known that Mr Castellini does not like to be talked to by normal people. Not without knowing what they are going to say. Under no circumstances must you talk to him unless he talks to you."

I took the photo out of my backpack. "Look, he

knows my mum. I think he might even like to speak to me."

Brussel didn't even look at the photo. He just said, "Trust me, kid, he wouldn't. Like I said, he doesn't *do* normal people."

Stan said, "This Mr Castellini sounds like a bit of a chump if you ask me."

And Ian said, "Who's he happy to talk to then – abnormal people?"

Brussel folded his arms. "He doesn't like to be surprised, that's all. Look, you'll get to speak to him when you introduce yourselves onstage, but don't go saying anything other than your names and why you're here, understand?"

Strictly speaking, as the reason I was there was to ask Paul Castellini to meet my mum, I wasn't lying when I said, "Yes, Brussel. I understand."

I think the first time I started to feel genuinely nervous and began to question EVERYTHING was when we were stood at the side of the stage and I heard the swell of applause as Paul Castellini walked up the steps to his piano. There must have been thousands of people in the studio. I don't think I had considered that there would be thousands of people watching me. Admittedly, this was a **MAHOOSIVE** oversight on my part. Especially considering that I had a pretty bad track record with public performances. After my pant-wetting-angel incident in the **Year Three nativity**, the time I became mute playing a cactus in **Oklahoma!** in Year Four, and the time I delivered the cactus lines I should have said in Year Four during a production of **Oliver!** in Year Five, I really should have thought about my plan more carefully.

My own fear was sidelined though when I looked at Sandesh. His face had completely paled, and his eyes were so wide that I was genuinely concerned they might fall out of his head.

"Are you okay?" I asked in a very trembly voice.

In an even more trembly voice, he said, "I'm just thinking that perhaps I don't want to be that interesting after all. Maybe I'm okay with boring. Boring seems like an alright kind of thing to be, you know?"

Another surge of applause came from the crowd and my stomach properly flip-flopped about like a dying mackerel. Sandesh might be right – boring did seem like a very good idea indeed.

We could have done a runner at that point. But we didn't. We stood paralysed as a very smiley Trixie Hawker bounced past us and onto the stage. After she had done a lot of bouncing and waving and whooping at the audience, she introduced Paul Castellini as the **"most magnificent singer of all time"**, which I think might have been a slight over-exaggeration, because I personally thought he sounded a bit warbly. Sandesh, however, stood with his mouth wide open and a look of pure admiration in his eyes.

When Paul Castellini had finished warbling, he took his seat in between the other two judges, smiled into the camera and flashed his overly-polished eyeballs down the lens.

And then Trixie Hawker whooped into her microphone, "I'm delighted to introduce our first **RECORD SMASHERS** to the show. Ladies and gentlemen, boys and girls, can you put your hands together for Lucy Robertson and Sandesh Agrawal!"

The crowd cheered and I did a little bit of sick in my mouth. Which I suppose, with all things considered, was better than peeing my pants.

CHAPTER 33

The tallest home-grown cactus is 33.5 m (What? That's three buses end to end!) and was grown in India

Before we knew it, Brussel had pushed us both onto the stage. My legs felt very strange, like they didn't belong to me. Not dissimilar to walking in flippers, come to think about it. The lights were blindingly bright and made even more dazzling because they were bouncing off our gold catsuits. I could barely bring myself to look at Sandesh, because the glare from his gold bum hurt my eyes so badly. It seemed possible that I was to become the first person with burned retinas from staring at someone's reflective backside.

But eye health was the least of my concerns, because when we reached the middle of the stage, the female judge sitting to Paul Castellini's left said, "Welcome to **RECORD SMASHERS**! I'm Za-Za Mallinderer. Can you tell the audience what treat you have in store for us today?"

And neither Sandesh nor I answered – not because we thought it was a rhetorical question, but because neither of us could remember how to speak. Which was a bit inconvenient.

Za-Za shifted in her seat and her long dangly earrings swung back and forth. She smiled at us again. "I know it can be nerve-racking, but take a deep breath and tell us what you are going to be doing."

Again, we stood there like a couple of mute cacti.

The woman on Paul Castellini's right-hand side, former daytime TV host Pamela Silverton, tried to have a go at getting us to speak too, but I was too mesmerized by her face to think about replying. It looked like she was standing in her own personal wind tunnel and her skin was being blasted off her skull.

She said, "You're going to be doing something remarkable with kumquats, isn't that right, Sandesh?"

Sandesh shifted from foot to foot and nodded.

And I thought, hang on a kumquat-gobbling minute! Sandesh wasn't going to be doing something remarkable with kumquats, *I was*. It was my plan – *I* was the one who was going to set a record and fix my mum.

Anyway, the injustice of being overlooked again seemed to activate my speaking muscles, because I said, "Ladies and gentlemen of the judgering panel. Ladies and gentlemen of the audience. I am Lucy Robertson and today, with the help of my friend and *co-performer* Sandesh" – I made sure I gave that bit the special emphasis it deserved – "I shall be setting a world record for catching **the most kumquats in my mouth ever in the world ever, EVER**. I shall be doing this in one minute and over a distance of ten metres. Ladies and gentlemen, boys and girls, do not try this at home because this is extremely dangerous and I am highly skilled."

I don't want to blow my own clarinet, but I think I did a very professional job. At that point anyway.

Sandesh was still being a bit useless so I shoved the punnet of kumquats into his hands and pushed him towards the far side of the stage.

I then turned back to Paul Castellini and said, "Mr Paul Castellini, would it be possible, before I start, for me to ask you one question?"

I stared deep into his shiny green eyes. It was the moment I had been waiting for. All I had to do was tell him who my mum was and invite him to be her happiness again.

He said, "I'll tell you what, I'm known for my mysterious nature and I like to keep it that way. But..." He pointed his finger at me. "I'll let you have one question and I promise to answer it absolutely truthfully." He stood up and looked around the audience, and for some reason the audience thought this was a very exciting prospect, because they all **oooooh**ed. And then he added, "But only IF you set a new record." The audience did an even bigger **oooooh** at that.

I could ask him a question, but I had to smash a record first? Way to load on the pressure, Paul.

I could have let it get to me, but at *that* point, I didn't. I just thought, *fine*, I'd smash the record and get my question. I gave Sandesh my most determined nod and said, "Sandesh...I. AM. READY!"

Sandesh placed the punnet of kumquats on top of the piano and held the first kumquat up so everyone could see. His trembling hands weren't exactly the picture of self-belief.

I positioned myself further down the stage with my mouth open, ready to catch. A man and woman in white suits came out carrying glittery clipboards. I guessed they were there in some official capacity to guarantee the record.

A loud drum roll boomed through the speakers. Both Sandesh and I jumped. And the audience laughed. The white-suited woman then shouted in quite an aggressive manner, "Record Smasher ready!"

I gave Sandesh a double thumbs-up and he pulled a very uncertain face.

I held my breath and tried to picture my mum's smile to give me confidence, but I just couldn't see it.

"Can I have a minute on the clock, please?" the official man said.

A big digital clock flashed up on the screen behind us. My heart began to beat triple time.

Then the whole audience counted down from three

and before I had a proper chance to prepare, we were off!

Sandesh threw the first kumquat, but it didn't go at all well. I think things were conspiring against us. The stage lights, the dazzling glare from our costumes, the rather terrifying number of people in the audience, the additional pressure old shiny-eyeballs had dumped on me, the fact that Sandesh's body seemed to be leaking sweat – there was a lot going on... And so the first kumquat didn't make it anywhere near my mouth. I hold Sandesh completely responsible for this, because the kumquat leaped out of his sweaty, slippery fingers and landed about twelve centimetres from his feet.

The audience laughed and white-suit lady stifled a snigger. Sandesh looked at me like a gold Lindt chocolate deer in the headlights. I shouted, "Quick, throw another!"

He sprang into action and started hurling kumquats at me at a lightning-fast rate. I can only blame myself for what happened next.

I didn't catch a single one.

I don't know what happened, other than I had completely lost all my kumquat-catching abilities. The **first** one hit me in the face, the **second** hit my neck, then the **third** and **fourth** hit the left and then right lens of my glasses, which made it even harder for me to see. I don't fully remember what happened after that, except that it felt like being paintballed with fruit.

I didn't catch a single kumquat in my mouth. Not one. Not even close. I just stood there being pelted by citrus. In front of the nation. Okay, so it wasn't the nation at the time, because the show hadn't been aired. I got the pleasure of experiencing my own humiliation at the same time as everybody else.

Anyway, I don't remember if the time ran out, or if Sandesh ran out of kumquats or if one of the celebrity judges called a stop to the massacre. But I do remember Paul Castellini leaning forward over his microphone and opening his mouth three times before saying, "Well, um, er, well…that was a bit unusual."

Pamela Silverton looked like she might be trying to frown but her face skin was fighting back. She said, "I'm not exactly sure what we've witnessed here but I'm pretty sure we haven't witnessed a record smasher."

I couldn't really argue with her about that.

Za-Za gave us a tight-lipped smile and said, "Thank you very much for your attempt. I'm sorry it didn't work out for you." Then she looked down at her clipboard and began to announce the next act. But I couldn't let that happen, because I hadn't asked Paul Castellini about my mum yet.

I said in rather a panicky voice, "Mr Castellini, before we go can I ask you something?"

I probably should have just said, "Mr Castellini, do you remember Lily Robertson? Do you think you might like to come and see her again?" but I didn't.

Paul said, "I believe I said I'd answer your question if you smashed a record. Did you smash a record?"

I shook my head and a bit of splattered kumquat fell out of my hair.

"Then I'm afraid unless you've got another record to try, we need to move on."

Again, I should have just blurted it out there and then, but up there, on that stage, with so much at stake, I simply could not think straight.

Brussel was madly waving at us to come off the stage. Two security men were loitering next to him.

It was then that I knew my whole entire plan had spectacularly failed.

It was over.

But then Sandesh said something **SOOOOOO** unexpected.

CHAPTER 34

The fastest sandwich made using bare feet was completed in 1 minute and 57 seconds by Rob Williams in the USA (bologna, cheese and lettuce – mmm!)

The three judges looked at each other and then turned back to Sandesh.

I said, "Sandesh, you want to do what?" because I couldn't have heard him correctly.

He took a step forward and placed his hands on his hips in a very superhero-type way and announced, "There's a record which I want to break, if you'll let me, Mr Castellini."

Za-Za twiddled her earrings and said, "It's your show, Paul, what do you think?"

Sandesh took another step forward. "Please, Mr Paul Castellini, it is very important that you permit me to attempt to smash this record."

Paul Castellini smoothed down his shirt. "Tell me, Sandeep, why is it so important?"

Sandesh swallowed hard and looked at me. "Because, Mr Castellini, it's very important to my very best friend, Lucy, that you let her ask her question. So important that she is willing to appear on national television covered in kumquat juice. And if it is important to her, then it's important to me, *Sandesh*."

Paul turned around to the audience and said, "Think we've got a little *friendship* unfolding in front of our eyes, don't you think?"

The whole crowd did a massive "**AWWW**" when he said that, and I blushed so much I think my cheeks actually started to sting.

"Well, who am I to stand in the way of young love?"

It was possible I was actually dying from cheek-heat at this point. There was absolutely nothing else left for me to do except self-combust from my face down.

Paul waved his arms theatrically. "Of course, Sandeep—"

"Sandesh."

"Sandesh, of course you shall be permitted to attempt to smash the world record for... I'm sorry, you're going to have to say it again because I'm not sure I completely took in what you're proposing."

"Thank you, Mr Castellini," Sandesh said and then addressed the audience in a very confident voice. "I, Sandesh Agrawal, am going to set the world record for **the most body parts used to play a song on the piano.**"

He did a big dramatic bow, then dropped into a low squat, bounced up and did a couple of lunges. Then he walked over to the grand piano, closed his eyes and took a deep, deep breath and the whole time I was thinking, *he's going to do what?*

He flexed his fingers as he sat down and – now I'm not a hundred per cent certain about this – but I think he turned to ME and said, "I shall be playing the number one hit by Mr Paul Castellini, *You Are My Happiness*."

Cue more furious blushing and some properly loud cheering from the crowd until they were all hushed into silence by the angry white-suit lady. Well, all except Stan and Ian, who carried on chanting things like "Go on, my son" and "You can do it, lad" and "Give it some welly", until white-suit lady threatened to chuck them out.

Because, for some inexplicable reason, I hadn't actually self-combusted from embarrassment, I was still standing in the centre of the stage, covered in kumquat juice and looking like a golden muppet. The logical thing would have been to run away from the scene. But I didn't. I stayed where I was and hoped that no one would notice me. Which seemed like a big ask, until Sandesh started playing.

After the first bar, I knew not a single person would be looking at me. Everyone was looking at him.

Because he was magnificent.

Truly spellbinding. He was clearly some kind of musical genius. And I'd never even bothered to hear him play before. What was that about?

His hands moved over the keyboard at incredible speed. The piano might seem boring to some people, but not the way he played it.

Especially when he started dropping in other body parts.

That's when his whole act was taken to another level.

A **record-smashing** level.

He used his elbow first – **plonk plonk plink** – without dropping a note.

That got a cheer.

Then his left foot: **plonkety plonk**. Then his right: **plink plonk plink**.

Bigger cheers.

His ear, his other elbow, his chin. Then his nose – **plink plink plonk plink plonk**. Loud cheers for that. His bum – **plunk**. Possibly the loudest cheer.

The judges were seat-dancing; Paul Castellini was mouthing the words and doing some hand actions. The crowd was loving it. *I* was loving it! Sandesh was smashing it!

And then, from out of nowhere, a door swung open at the back of the auditorium and in bowled Aunty Sheila, flanked by two police officers and about forty other people – most of whom I didn't know but they looked like they had come straight from an Indian wedding. And behind them all was my mum.

CHAPTER 35

The piano piece played with the most body parts was performed by Sandesh Agrawal in the UK

Aunty Sheila stormed down the aisle between the seats, her flowery kaftan billowing behind her like a superhero's cape. Mum was right next to her, her cardigan wrapped tightly around her, her eyes locked on mine. The two security men spotted them and tried to stand in their way, but pretty much bounced off their angry-lady forcefield and then were ploughed over by a lot of furious-looking wedding guests led by Sandesh's dada and dadi and a man and woman who could have only been his mum and dad.

Quite honestly, it was one of the most alarming sights I'd ever seen. I could tell by the looks on Aunty

Sheila's and Mum's faces that we were in trouble.

So much trouble. Sandesh didn't notice, he was

too busy playing the final few bars of

"*You Are My Happiness*", with

his bum and his left elbow – **plunk

plonkety plink**!

It was only when he finished his final note to rapturous applause and Aunty Sheila, Mum and the others clambered up onto the stage that he realized what was going on around him and that we'd been caught. That put a stop to all his bowing. When he clocked his dadi standing there with her arms crossed and a questioning look on her face, he seemed to shrink down inside his gold costume. Then he looked even more worried when he saw his mum and dad. He said, "Mum, I can explain."

But he didn't need to – which was probably a good job, as it would have taken a while – because his mum ran over to him, cupped his face in her hands and said, "Sandesh, that was phenomenal! I've never seen anything...I mean...technically you were perfect, but the passion – you can't teach that! What did you think, Nandish?"

Sandesh's dad said, "I'm beyond proud, son."

Before Sandesh had a chance to reply, Paul Castellini shouted, "Wow! Just wow! What an ending! We love a family act here on **RECORD SMASHERS**!" He clearly thought the stage invasion had been prearranged.

"I have never seen such a display. Everything about it was perfect. From your playing to your choice of song! That was magnificent, but was it a world record?"

Because Aunty Sheila wasn't wearing a microphone, no one except me heard her say, "I don't care if it is a record, Mr Perma Tan. Can someone explain to me why these *children* are here unaccompanied?"

I felt someone slip their hand into mine. Mum. I looked at her and her eyes looked brighter than they had in the weeks before she went into hospital, and I couldn't help but smile. She smiled back – although she still looked a bit concerned/cross – and said, "Lucy, I've been so worried. When Sheila called to say you hadn't turned up at the wedding, I didn't know what to think."

I didn't say anything, I was too busy just looking at her.

She stroked my cheek with her hand and said, "Poppet, what on earth's going on? Why are you onstage in Aunty Sheila's ABBA outfit? And why are you so sticky?"

I did not have time at that moment to explain about

the kumquat juice, or the gold catsuit, or the reason I was on the stage of **RECORD SMASHERS**, because right at that very moment I just had to hug her. And I think she had to hug me too, because she wrapped her arms around me so tightly that it almost hurt, but I didn't care because she squeezed some of the sadness out.

I could have stayed like that for ever, but when Paul Castellini's voice boomed over the microphone I suddenly remembered where I was.

Paul was pointing at the white-suit people. "Can you confirm if that's a record?"

White-suit man looked at his clipboard and then whispered into angry white-suit lady's ear. She looked at her clipboard and then looked at the audience and said, "I can confirm that was indeed a **RECORD SMASHER**!"

When she said that, loads of gold confetti dropped down on us from the ceiling. The crowd cheered, but

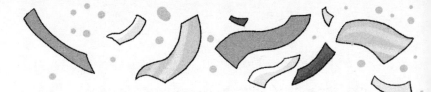

everyone on the stage stood there looking either angry-confused (Aunty Sheila and Sandesh's relatives) or terrified-worried (Sandesh) or happy (me and Mum).

When all the noise had died down, Aunty Sheila grabbed the microphone that was taped to my front and said, "Can someone please explain why unaccompanied minors have been permitted to perform for this incredibly exploitative show without permission from a parent or guardian?"

Which was a total and utter **BUZZKILL**.

Paul, Za-Za and Pamela looked very uncomfortable when she said that. I suppose I'm used to being told off by a pink-haired lady in a billowy kaftan, but they probably weren't. Brussel ran onto the stage, waving a piece of paper. "But we have permission. From the dads."

Everyone turned to look at Stan and Ian, who were now standing right at the edge of the stage.

Aunty Sheila looked at Mum. Mum looked at me and I looked at Sandesh. Then Aunty Sheila said, "Who, in the love of all things fixable, are they?"

Sandesh didn't answer. I didn't answer. But one of the police who had turned up with Aunty Sheila answered. She said, "That's Stan and Ian Trunkle."

And that's when Stan and Ian Trunkle legged it.

CHAPTER 36

The fastest police car in service is the Bugatti Veyron with a top speed of 407 km/h, used by police in Dubai

It's very hard to recall the exact order of how things played out then, because it was complete and utter chaos, but I think it went something a bit like this.

Za-Za was on her feet, her earrings swinging about madly, shouting, "Security! Security! Security!" Which seemed unnecessary when the police were already involved, and a little bit annoying, if I'm honest.

Pamela had sunk down in her seat with her hand on her chest and was making a low wailing noise like a rubbish ghost. Her face remained absolutely motionless, so it was quite hard to work out what was going on there.

Then the police that Aunty Sheila had commandeered were suddenly up on the stage to the left of me and shouting, "Stop where you are, Trunkle brothers!"

But Stan and Ian didn't stop. They said some very rude words as they darted across the stage towards the fire escape. They were surprisingly quick on their feet for their size. As Ian passed me, he pressed something into my hand. Our eyes locked for a teeny tiny fraction of a millisecond. "Look after Mum for us, kid," he whispered.

As the police ran by me, I considered dive-tackling them to give our fake dads a chance to escape. Luckily I didn't have to, because when they hit a patch of squashed kumquats they both fell over, giving Stan and Ian vital seconds. The Trunkles burst out through the fire doors and a really loud alarm started to ring, which only added to the pandemonium.

The police struggled to their feet, but as they ran past Sandesh they stacked it again. Somehow the piano stool was pushed forward just at the wrong time and because the police were not semi-professional hurdlers like me, they both tripped over and landed on their faces.

Sandesh made a properly good show of apologizing and kept saying, "I'm so sorry. I did not mean to do that." But after he had helped pull them to their feet, he winked at me and I KNEW he had done it on purpose. He really was being exceptionally heroic.

The police disappeared out of the fire escape and thankfully someone turned off the wailing alarm.

I looked at Sandesh and he mouthed, "I hope they get away."

I did too, but I didn't fancy their chances.

All this time, I'd sort of forgotten that we were still being watched by the judges and a huge studio audience. I only remembered when Paul Castellini said, in a loud and slightly angry voice, "Seeing as everything is under control now, could we please get back to the show?" I don't think he liked being forgotten about.

Paul managed to slap a smile on his face as he turned to Sandesh. "So how does it feel to be a **RECORD SMASHER**, Sandeep?"

All forty-odd members of Sandesh's family said at the same time, "It's SANDESH!"

Sandesh looked at his parents, then turned back to Paul Castellini and said, "It feels very good, thank you, Mr Castellini. But if you wouldn't mind, could we get to the bit where Lucy gets to ask her question?"

Paul rubbed his hands together. I think he was pleased things were about him again. He said, "Ah, of course, the question. Fire away, young lady."

I looked at Mum, then I looked at Paul Castellini, then I looked at Mum again and then she pulled a face and said, "Lucy, what are you doing?" Like she knew I was up to something.

I let out a deep breath and went for it. "Mr Paul Castellini, this is my mum, Lily Robertson, and I think you might just be the answer to her happiness. I think you made her happy once, because there's this photo of you both, see –" I grabbed it out of my backpack and held it up – "when you were both friends. And on the back of it some words are written. And do you know what the words say? Well, they say *You are my happiness*. And you're both smiling and Mum looks happy. And I want her to be happy. And if it is you who can make her happy and keep her from feeling sad,

292

then I really think you ought to come over to ours for your tea. Do you like lasagne? If not, Aunty Sheila's got a lot of ox tongues and sardines. I'm sorry, I think I asked more than one question there. So could you maybe just answer the coming-over-for-your-tea question?"

I don't think I've heard silence like it before. It was so silent. Which was amazing, considering I was standing in a huge auditorium with thousands of people watching. It was like someone had pressed pause on everything but me.

As Paul hadn't answered and no one else was speaking, I began to wonder if I had said it all in my head and not out loud. I was about to start the whole speech again, probably without mentioning sardines and ox tongues, but Paul said, "I'm sorry, kid. I've never seen that woman before in my life. There must be some mistake."

I looked at Mum and she had this look on her face which at first I thought was sadness but, looking back now, I think was actually worry. She put her hand on my shoulder and said, "Oh, Lucy. Is that what all this is about? I...I...sweetheart, I really don't know what to say."

"I wanted to find your happiness, Mum. And he's sitting right there." I grabbed her and pushed her forward. "Look at her again, Mr Castellini, you must know her. Please."

Paul looked at my mum, hesitated, then said, "I'm sorry. I really don't think I've ever met you."

Mum closed her eyes for a second and shook her head. When she opened them again, she said, "We did meet once, but I'd never expect you to remember." She turned to me. "Lucy, I don't know Paul Castellini. Your Aunty Sheila and I went to watch him on his '*You Are My Happiness*' tour years ago. We got to go backstage and take a photo with him because Aunty Sheila had collected coupons off a load of tins of chicken-and-mushroom soup."

Aunty Sheila moved to stand next to me and very quietly said, "One thousand and sixteen coupons, if I remember correctly."

Mum squeezed my shoulder. "Paul Castellini is not the answer to my happiness, Lucy. And you should not be the one trying to look for it—"

She carried on talking but I wasn't really listening, because the sheer enormity of my mistake was beginning to dawn on me. Everything had been for nothing. Wilbur, the pegs, the hurdling in flippers, the kumquats...*everything* had been a waste of time.

I looked down at my shiny gold belly and felt incredibly and completely stupid. I wanted to run away back to Aunty Sheila's and hide right at the bottom of my canoe. But then I realized that I was still holding onto something.

I opened my hand and looked down at the car key

Ian had pressed into my hand. I knew instantly what I had to do. I might have failed my mum, but I could at least still help Mrs Trunkle.

CHAPTER 37

The world's largest car park holds 20,000 cars and is in Canada – but, at the time, the one at the RECORD SMASHERS studio felt like it might be bigger

I couldn't stand on that stage a second longer, so I weaved in and out of all the people and raced over to Sandesh. I grabbed hold of his hand and pulled him down the steps, through the side door, back through the warren of corridors and finally out into the car park.

He didn't question why I'd just dragged him away from his family, who were more than likely to be hot on our heels, until we were outside, and then he said, "Is everything okay, Lucy?"

I meant to tell him about the key Ian had given me and my new plan, but I found different words coming out of my mouth, which were, "You were amazing. What you did out there – I mean, it was incredible. Your playing, all those different body parts...I mean, wow. Truly, wow."

He couldn't quite look at me when he said, "I wasn't boring then?"

"Sandesh, you were only interesting. You are always only interesting. You are the most interesting person I know and my best friend. My only proper friend, I suppose, but if I had any other proper ones, you'd definitely still be the best."

At that point, I began to think I'd gone a bit too far. It was true – he was the most interesting person I knew and my best friend – but still... Maybe I should have gone with a simple, "Well done on your record." I tried to ignore the sudden awkwardness I was feeling, but he only went and stared me straight in the eyes and said, "And you are the most interesting person I know too, and you are also my best friend."

I smiled and then I blushed and then I tried to speak, but all the words got jumbled up in my teeth.

Sandesh didn't seem to mind though. He said,

"Did you hear what my mum said? She said I was phenomenal."

"She did. And Paul Castellini thought so too."

"You know what, Lucy? If you'd told me that this morning I would have been ecstatic, but now I'm not sure I'm such a big fan of his any more."

I nudged him. "I can understand why, *Sandeep*."

He laughed, then looked down and said, "Lucy, why am I standing in the car park in a gold catsuit?" Which brought me back to the moment.

"Ah! Quick!" I shoved the car key under his nose. "This key! Mother Trunkle! Come on!"

Understandably, he looked a bit confused. I'll admit, it wasn't the most detailed of explanations, so I said, "We've got to help Mrs Trunkle before all of the mortgage company people throw her out of her house!"

"But how are we going to do that?"

It was a fair-enough question, but luckily I had it all worked out.

"We've got to get to the painting before the police do and sell it and then give the money to Stan and Ian's mum so she can stay in her home."

And even though very recent experience didn't exactly suggest I have a superb track record with plans, Sandesh said, "That's an awesome plan!"

We raced around, trying to remember where we had parked the car. All we could come up with was that it was white – like a thousand other cars in the car park. After a lot more running around, eventually Sandesh thought to use the clicker. We spotted the car's lights flashing and dived towards it.

I flung the back door open and was just about to pull the painting out when the driver's door opened and Aunty Sheila stuck her head in. Then the front passenger door opened too and Mum popped her head in and they both said, "Lucy, what on earth are you doing now? Why did you run away like that?"

I looked up and through the windscreen I could see the two policemen heading in our direction. I gasped and said, "Oh no! Not the police. We need to bust outta here." Which I think sounded quite exciting.

Mum said, "Lucy, we're not going to bust out of anywhere. We need to talk about what happened."

And Aunty Sheila said, "I think you need to explain EXACTLY what is going on here."

We were running out of time, so I said, "Mum, Aunty Sheila, please trust me. There is something very important I need to do for Ian and Stan, but I can't go through it all right now."

I gazed at Mum and then at Aunty Sheila with my best pleading eyes and they both looked at each other.

Aunty Sheila said, "There's no way we're going to let you get caught up in the exploits of a couple of criminals. No way."

"Please, Aunty Sheila, you're the one who told me not to judge people without getting to know them."

"I didn't mean thieves, Lucy!"

"They're not really proper thieves, are they, Sandesh?"

Sandesh stuck his head in through the other back door and said, "Actually, they are thieves, but like Robin Hood of Sherwood Forest rather than proper ones."

Aunty Sheila sighed loudly. "I do not believe what I am hearing."

I could see the police were looking down Row F of

the car park. We were in J – we didn't have long. I looked at Mum again. "Please, Mum. Can you do this for me? Just this one thing? I didn't manage to make you happy, but maybe, just maybe I can help Mrs Trunkle."

Mum clasped her hand over her mouth and for a moment I thought she was going to cry. But she didn't. Instead she took a deep breath and said, "Lucy, darling, it is not your responsibility to make me happy. Things are complicated, feelings are complicated, but what is not complicated is how much I love you and how proud I am of you. Do you understand?"

And I think, for the first time, I did.

Then she said – and I think she *was* crying a bit now, but not in a sad way, in a *happy* way – "Whatever it is, Lucy, my brave, brave girl, I'll do it. Look at what you were willing to do for me! You went onstage in a gold costume so you could invite Paul Castellini – of all people – round to ours for lasagne! This really is the least I can do."

Aunty Sheila shouted, "Lily! What are you thinking?"

And in a very determined voice that made my tummy

tingle, Mum said, "I'm thinking that my daughter has asked me to do something and I would like to do it for her. I would like to do it for her very much. I haven't been able to do a lot for her recently, but I can do this."

I started to pull the painting out of the back door. It was pretty heavy. "We need to take this package back to ours."

"What is it?" Aunty Sheila asked. "It's not drugs or a bomb or something catastrophic, is it?"

I rolled my eyes. "Does it look like any of those things?"

She grabbed hold of one end and said, "Less of your cheek, young lady. Now where did I park the van?"

Sandesh and Mum slammed the car doors and grabbed a corner each and we all half-walked, half-ran to where Aunty Sheila had parked the van. Sandesh and I jumped in the back, slotting the painting between the glittery loo seats and the meerkat dolls, and Mum and Aunty Sheila climbed in the front. We screeched out of the car park past the police, which was actually rather exhilarating. But when Aunty Sheila saw a big group of Sandesh's family members standing at the entrance of the car park, she slammed on the brakes sharply, wound the window down and called over to Sandesh's mum and dad.

"Mr and Mrs Agrawal! Just so you know, we have Sandesh. We have a slight situation, that we really need to attend to."

"A situation?" Sandesh's mum said.

Sandesh opened the back door of the van. "Don't worry, Mum. This is just something I've got to do."

Sandesh's dad took a step forward like he was going to say he couldn't come with us, but Sandesh's mum put her hand on his arm. "Nandish, if Sandesh tells us there is something he has to do, I think we have learned that it is best if we let him."

I could only see the back of Sandesh's head but I could tell by the way he shouted, "Thanks, Mum. I love you. See you later!" that he was smiling.

"We'll deliver him back safely after he's had his tea," Aunty Sheila said. "Lovely to meet you today!"

She put her foot back on the accelerator and we shot off just as Sandesh closed the back door. Then she shouted over her shoulder at me, "Right, Lucy, I think it might be a good time to explain why we seem to be handling stolen property."

When I had finished telling them about Stan and Ian and the painting and the mortgage people and Mrs Trunkle, Aunty Sheila tightened her pink ponytail and said, "Well, okay then. This family is not the sort of family that allows a big corporation to push a defenceless old lady out of her home."

Mum pulled at her seat belt so she could turn around and look at me and said, "Lucy, you have such a big heart and you make me very happy."

My very big heart almost burst right there and then.

CHAPTER 38

The longest-reigning living queen is Her Majesty Queen Elizabeth II

We all stood around the kitchen table, looking at the package like it might actually be an unexploded bomb.

Aunty Sheila said, "I think I need a drink," opened the fridge door and poured herself a shot of aloe vera juice, then knocked it back.

Mum said, "What is it a painting of?"

"We don't actually know. Just that it's valuable."

Aunty Sheila poured herself another little glass of green slime and said, "Are you sure you're up to this, Lily?"

Mum said, "I'm fine," in a way that made me believe

her, and then she said, "I just want to be here to help my daughter for once."

"Are you out of hospital for good now, Mum?" I asked, trying not to sound too hopeful so she wouldn't feel bad if the answer was no.

She squeezed my hand. "Not quite, but soon. Next week. And Evelyn, at the hospital, would like you to visit next week for us to have our first session all together then. Would that be okay for you, Lucy?"

"That would be more than okay, Mum." I squeezed her hand back and we smiled at each other and it felt really good.

Eventually I let go of her hand and said, "Shall we have a look?" I ripped the corner of the brown paper and through the tear we could see bright orange.

"That's a very modern colour," Mum said.

Sandesh helped me pull the rest of the paper off to reveal the picture. We all knew what it was immediately.

Aunty Sheila wiped the green juice off her top lip with the back of her sleeve and gasped. "Well I never. A genuine Andy Warhol portrait of our Queen!"

Sandesh said, "Ahhh, AWP – Andy Warhol Painting!

Not the Arctic animal Welfare Patrol at all!"

Mum said, "Arctic what?"

And he said, "Never mind."

It was then that I realized Aunty Sheila looked very excited. She leaped to her feet and said, "I'll buy it! How much is it?"

I frowned. "Aunty Sheila, this is an expensive painting, not a job lot of Henry Hoovers. You can't buy this. You'd have to be rich."

Aunty Sheila said, "But I am rich."

I sighed. "Yes, I know you're rich in all the ways that count, like love and friends and family and health and sardines and ox tongues, but you're not rich as in money rich."

She smiled. "Why do you think I'm not rich as in money rich?"

"I sleep in a canoe, for starters. You live in a tiny house and everything you buy has been owned before and your clothes all come from charity shops and your van is over thirty years old and—"

Her smile got bigger. "But that is why I *am* money rich."

Sandesh seemed to be buying it, because he said, "Seriously? You're rich, Aunty Sheila?"

"I'm loaded because I've been careful and I don't waste."

"You also made an absolute killing on the stock market a few years back," Mum reminded her.

This was very unexpected news. "Why have I been sleeping in a plastic boat all this time?"

"Didn't you enjoy it?" Aunty Sheila asked. "Not everybody gets to sleep in a canoe."

I said, "There's a reason for that. And it's beds!"

She smiled and said, "You had your adventure though, didn't you?"

Mum stroked my cheek and said, "She certainly did."

In the end it was Mum and Aunty Sheila who came up with a plan. Aunty Sheila rang up the police station and told them we had come into possession of the stolen painting but refused to say how. It turned out there was a reward, which Aunty Sheila immediately gave to Mrs

Trunkle to pay off the mortgage people. Mrs Trunkle was very grateful and when Mum told her that it was from Ian and Stan, Mrs Trunkle cried and laughed and hugged us all.

After Aunty Sheila had spoken to the police, she got the number for the person who owned the painting. Except it didn't turn out to be a person. The Trunkles hadn't lied when they said it belonged to a faceless corporation. Anyway, the painting was usually kept in a safe in a bank somewhere and not hung on a wall – which Aunty Sheila said was more of a criminal act than anything Stan and Ian had ever done. So she bought it.

And now it hangs above my canoe in the sitting room.

Aunty Sheila says she loves it because of the colour and that it's a little bit of all of us – her, Mum, even me. She says we're all queens in our own way.

But to me, the orange colour will always remind me of kumquats. And kumquats will always remind me of Sandesh.

CHAPTER 39

The most valuable thing in the world is happiness

The evening that the first **RECORD SMASHERS** episode aired, it seemed only right that Mum, Aunty Sheila, Sandesh, his parents and his grandparents and I watched it together. Obviously, we brought Wilbur along too. He had a bit of a funky smell and was getting a bit squishy on one side, but I'd put a plaster on him, and it seemed to do the trick.

It was a little cramped in Aunty Sheila's living room, but no one minded. Sandesh's family squished up on the three-seater sofa, Mum and Aunty Sheila sat on the floor and Sandesh and I sat in my canoe.

After Sandesh's dada had performed some magic

tricks which weren't that magical as a warm-up for the main show, we watched a video of Paul Castellini's *"You Are My Happiness"* concert. Aunty Sheila is the only person on the planet to own an old video-tape player. Well, actually, she has two.

Sandesh said, "I know I'm not *such* a huge fan of his any more, but it is still pretty cool that I got to perform for Paul Castellini. I won't ever forget it."

Aunty Sheila said, "I doubt that Paul Castellini will ever forget it either."

Mum said, "You really were extremely entertaining, Sandesh."

And Sandesh's mum said, "I predict a brilliant musical career for you – that is, if you want it."

Sandesh did a very big smile at that and said, "I did enjoy performing."

While we listened to warbly old Castellini, a thought dropped into my head. "What I don't understand, Aunty Sheila, is how you knew we were at the **RECORD SMASHERS** studio. It's almost like you had a tracker on us or something."

Aunty Sheila cleared her throat and said, "Don't be

ridiculous," in a way that made me think I was not being at ALL ridiculous by mentioning a tracker.

I said, "Aunty Sheila, do you have a tracker on me?"

She said, "Does anyone want some yoghurt?"

I wasn't going to be fooled by her terrible attempt at distraction, so I said, "Aunty Sheila!" in my most sternest of voices, which seemed to do the trick, because she said, "Fine, yes. But aren't you glad I do – I mean, did?"

"Where?!"

"I put them in all your shoes. I did try sewing them into your knickers, but they didn't survive the washing-machine spin cycle."

"What?!"

"I thought the shoe one had gone on the blink too after I watched your location circling a roundabout fourteen times in Luton."

"But why?!"

"In case something terrible happened. You are very precious, Lucy, and it is only right that people keep an eye on their precious things."

I didn't quite know what to say to that, because while

I thought she had probably violated my human rights by secretly tracking me, I was also delighted about being called precious.

But then she sighed and said, "You know what? Maybe I need to learn to stop worrying about all the bad things that might happen and start to enjoy all the good things that are happening right now."

When the concert had finished, we turned on the TV for the first ever episode of **RECORD SMASHERS**. The entire kumquat-catching attempt had been cut down to twelve seconds and was featured in a selection of clips called "**RECORD FAILURES**". Believe me, twelve seconds was more than long enough. I had to peek out from behind Wilbur while tiny TV me was hit repeatedly in the face by kumquats.

Sandesh said, "It's remarkable – you didn't even move. I don't think you even blinked."

I could tell everyone in the room was trying not to laugh. Aunty Sheila just grinned and said, "Awww. Never mind."

Mum winked at me. "Darling, I'm still very proud of you for trying and I'll never forget why you did what you did. In fact, I'll remember it every time I look at a kumquat."

Then they pulled out a couple of clothes pegs from their pockets and clipped them to their cheeks. I think this was them trying to tease me, but I rose above it and ignored them.

Sandesh's TV bit was longer than mine, but not by much, which seemed a bit unfair considering he actually set a new record. There were only twenty-two seconds of him being extraordinary on the piano. I guess too much of his performance was ruined by the events that followed.

Anyway, to make up for it we all whooped very loudly during his bit, and even though his cheeks flushed, he did stand up when Aunty Sheila ordered him to take a bow. After his first bow we all stomped our feet and clapped really hard, so he bowed again, and we did it some more. And then he bowed again and again. It almost got a bit too much, to be honest, but he finally stopped when his dad said, "I think we have a new star in the family. That was longer than one of your curtain calls, Jayani."

Sandesh's mum laughed and said, "He deserves it!"

Sandesh sat back down next to me in the canoe and whispered, "I bet Billy Griggs didn't do anything *that* interesting this holiday."

I said, "I am absolutely one hundred per cent certain he didn't."

During the credits, Sandesh's family went back next door, but he decided to stay a while longer. He disappeared to the kitchen to get us some squash. When he came back, he was holding a tray of drinks and my Campian ED10 camera. He put the tray on top

of the box of flamingos and said, "Sheila, Lucy, Lily –
photo time."

I shook my head. "It doesn't work. I didn't manage
to fix it."

But he didn't listen and said, "Let's just try it anyway."

Aunty Sheila and Mum came and squashed into the
canoe and each put an arm around me.

Sandesh pressed the button and, by some miracle,
the camera worked.

He looked at the screen and said, "Great photo."

"Give that here. That shouldn't work. It's broken."

I looked at the screen and saw it had worked but
that Sandesh had not in fact taken a photo of us, but
one of his own face, with his trademark massive smile.

"You're right," I said. "It is a great photo." I shoved
the camera back in his hands. "Now do it properly."

He took another picture and held it up for me to see.

"You look very joyous, Lucy. Very happy."

And when I looked at myself, I realized he was right.
Those photos of Sandesh, and of me, Mum and Aunty
Sheila in my canoe, are my favourite ever photos now.
I keep them under my pillow and when times get tricky

and Mum's sadness creeps back, which it sometimes does, I like to look at them and remember that moment.

Sandesh, with his huge record-smashing heart.

And Mum and Aunty Sheila, with pegs clipped to their cheeks and wearing their happiness on the outside.

Mum is smiling, really smiling, from the freckles on her nose, all the way down to the tips of her outstretched fingers.

And so am I.

The first time I saw that photo of the three of us, I realized something when I looked at myself. For the first time, in a long time, I looked truly happy. And that's when it hit me. The whole time I'd been trying to get onto **RECORD SMASHERS**, I thought I'd been searching for my mum's happiness. But I was wrong about that.

I'd really been searching for mine.

I suppose I thought Mum being well would be the answer to my happiness. But I was wrong about that too. Of course I want Mum to be happy, but now I'm happy with her just being her.

I guess what I've realized is that you can't hinge

your own happiness onto one person or one thing. Happiness comes from a lot of different places.

You just have to notice them.

It could come from a bag of shrimps (the sweets, not the freshwater prawns), or from a watermelon named Wilbur. From a backie to the newsagent's, or from a friend who is willing to wear a spangly gold costume in public for you. From an aunty who will sew a tracker into your knickers because she is scared of everything and yet nothing all at once. From music and art and from criminals with big hearts and from helping others and from family in all its forms. And from mums, even if sometimes they feel a little bit broken. Because even broken things can be incredible.

I still don't know why the Campian ED10 camera worked that day. I had tried everything I could think of to fix it – I'd pulled it apart, put it back together, shouted at it, cried over it, even thrown it across the room – and nothing had helped. I asked if Aunty Sheila had fixed it, but she said no and so did Sandesh.

I wonder now if just leaving it alone meant it somehow fixed itself.

Don't get me wrong – it's still not perfect. Sometimes it stops working and I start to get cross and annoyed because I can't work out why. I sometimes think about chucking it away and buying a new one. But then I remember, even though it might be a little bit broken, it is still capable of producing the most incredible pictures and capturing the happiest of memories.

Aunty Sheila would probably say that's a bit like people. And I think she'd be right about that. Because what I've learned is that just because you *want* to fix something, it doesn't mean you can, and it doesn't mean you should.

THE END

A NOTE FROM JENNY

Dear Reader,

I believe all emotions exist for a purpose – they are what make us human. We need to feel happy and joyful, silly and daft and, sometimes, we need to feel sad. Because there are things which happen in our lives that are sad.

What I don't think you ever need to feel is alone.

But this is what can happen when, like Lucy, you have a parent or guardian with a mental health illness. The truth is though, that one in four people experience mental health problems every year. And this means there are a lot of people whose lives are touched by mental illness.

Maybe we don't realize that because we're not always very good at talking about it.

I have learned that when you don't talk about the things that you are finding difficult, they can become bigger, scarier and more powerful. In turn, you can start to feel smaller and you can also feel like the only person in the world who is going through what you're going through. It is when you share your feelings with others that you realize that is not the case, and you are never alone.

If, like Lucy, you love someone with a mental health illness and are finding things hard, I want you to know that there are people you can talk to.

Lucy is fortunate that she has Aunty Sheila to talk to. You might feel like you don't have anyone to talk to, but remember you are not alone. Speak to a trusted teacher, a relation or your GP.

There are also charities and organisations who are able to help. On the next page, you can find details for Childline, who have a helpline for young people available every day, where you can talk to a trained counsellor, as well as further ways in which you can contact them and talk about anything worrying you.

Or there is also the wonderful charity Our Time who help young people affected by parental mental illness. There is more information about the work they do on the next page, and they have a useful Get Help section on their website too.

And, above all, please remember, you are not alone.

Jenny Pearson

Our Time

Helping young people affected by parental mental illness

Our Time is a charity that helps young people whose parents have a mental illness by increasing their resilience.

When a parent suffers from mental illness it is rare for anyone – parent, teacher, or even social worker – to know how to discuss the illness with the child. The children are often confused and frightened. In England alone, it's estimated that 2.9 million children and young people live with a parent who has reported symptoms of anxiety and depression – and that figure doesn't capture the whole of the UK. At present most receive no support. Our Time provides interventions for families and in schools to support these young people to ensure they get the right help early on and prevent them from becoming patients themselves.

Visit **www.ourtime.org.uk** for more information.

How to be a RECORD SMASHER, with Guinness World Records

Have Lucy and Sandesh inspired you to try breaking a world record? It's a **SMASHING** thing to attempt, and you could win yourself fame and fortune, or at the very least, something to say when you have to introduce yourself with a fun fact.

It's important to tackle your record smashing with care and attention, however, so here are some top record-smashing tips from the experts at **GUINNESS WORLD RECORDS** to set you up for success.

1. Take Your Pick

There are currently over **40,000 Guinness World Records titles**, so there is no shortage of records to pick from – or you could even invent a new one, like Lucy and Sandesh did. You can also find some records specially created for budding smashers at: **kids.guinnessworldrecords.com**.

REMEMBER: you'll need to apply to Guinness World Records **BEFORE** you make your attempt, so that they can send you the guidelines and make sure your effort counts!

2. Tell a Grown-up

You will need an adult to help you apply for your record. They can really take your attempt to the next level too – they can help you to reach high shelves, drive you places, maybe even pay for supplies. Find someone willing to get involved, such as a parent or guardian, a teacher or an Aunty Sheila. Check that they're happy with your chosen record before you apply to break it.

3. Risk Assess

If you plan for all possible mishaps, you'll give yourself the best chance at record smashing. Think of anything that could go wrong, and adapt your plan to minimize the risks. If there's a problem you can't find a way around, consider picking a different record. After all, Lucy and Sandesh would never have discovered their kumquat talents if they hadn't wisely moved away from sword-juggling.

4. Be Prepared

Not just for Scouts. Carefully read the guidelines Guinness World Records send you and follow them to the letter, or else risk the dreaded disqualification! Video your record attempt and make sure you've got some grown-ups on hand to act as witnesses. Do not expect to break a record on your first try – if it was that easy, everyone would have one. But if you pick wisely, practise hard and really throw yourself into it – no, don't literally throw yourself into anything, haven't you listened to any of my safety tips? – there's no reason you can't join the elite group of **Incredible Record Smashers**.

And you can find RECORD SMASHING tips, facts and much more over at kids.guinnessworldrecords.com!

Jenny Pearson's FIVE FAVOURITE WORLD RECORDS...

1. Sweet Pea the Wonder Dog!

This dog has actually broken three records! What is life when a dog is doing better than you? Anyway, Sweet Pea, an Australian shepherd/ Border collie mix, not only walked up ten steps while balancing a five-ounce glass of water on her head, she also walked down ten steps without spilling a drop and then went on to win the title for fastest 100m with a can on her head. I'd like to see Usain Bolt beat that one! Good girl, Sweet Pea, good girl!

2. The Largest Human Mattress Dominoes

Yes, it's a thing! An amazing thing! The folks at Globo Comunicação e Participações S.A. and Ortobom really know how to have a good time. I would have loved to have been part of this record-smashing! Two thousand and nineteen people strapped themselves to mattresses and toppled into one another in a domino chain. What a sight to behold that must have been! And the lovely thing is that the mattresses were later donated to charity.

3. Most Pinky Pull-Ups

A pull-up is an important life skill and one I don't have. My inability to do a single pull-up is a constant worry because I wonder what would happen to me if I ever ended up dangling off a cliff. Anyway, a pinky pull-up is using only your little fingers to hoist yourself skywards – doesn't seem possible, right? Wrong! Tazio Gavioli managed thirty-six of them! Unbelievable – those be some powerful pinkies! What's even more smashing about this record is that Tazio dedicated it to his cat Kali, who inspired him after losing a paw in an accident.

4. Most Toothpicks in a Beard

Joel Strasser stuck a whopping 3,500 toothpicks into his beard. I find this especially impressive for two reasons: 1. That's an awful lot of toothpicks 2. Growing a beard is really very difficult. I certainly have not managed it yet, so kudos to Joel.

5. Most Canned Drinks Opened by a Parrot in One Minute

Now, I don't know if there are a lot of parrots in training for this, but it's not the number of competitors that is important, it is the achievement itself that counts. And what an achievement! Zac the macaw managed to open thirty-five cans of pop in sixty seconds to claim his world record and make all other can-openers look, frankly, boring in comparison.

Find out lots more about the SMASHING Jenny Pearson at www.jennypearsonauthor.com

ACKNOWLEDGEMENTS

I just have to take this opportunity to acknowledge JUST HOW INCREDIBLE Rebecca Hill is. Not only as an editor, but as an all-round amazing human being and I will always feel so excited and terribly lucky that I get to work with her.

I would also like to thank her kids, Big G and Little R for their support. They are, undoubtedly, a couple of legends!

Erica Salcedo has brought Lucy and Sandesh's story to life with more humour and joy than I could ever have imagined. Every single illustration fills me with happiness – thank you so much.

Thanks to Andrew for picking up the slack and keeping me fed and watered, to my children William and Douglas, who have conditioned me to be able to write anywhere, no matter how noisy or chaotic. And to my dad and Eleanor for forcing my books onto everybody they know!

Under the phenomenal family duo that is Peter and Nicola, the whole team at Usborne is frankly smashing it out of the park with the books they are publishing. So huge thanks to everyone for working on mine. I'm so proud to be an Usborne author.

Special thanks to the brilliant Becky Walker for being so much fun to work with. I cannot believe you already had a Wilbur the Watermelon in your life. And, editorially, you are Just. So. Good.

To Leila Rasheed, I am unbelievably grateful for your insight, truly, I cannot thank you enough.

Jo Olney, you creative goddess, you! Your ideas and talent constantly amaze me, and you send the best emails.

Katarina Jovanovic and Fritha Lindqvist, I am so grateful for all you do, pushing me and my books out into the world. You are both stars!

To Penelope Mazza, thank you for your incredibly inspiring

book trailer, which has had so many views and frankly I don't care if they were all me because I LOVE it so much.

To Katharine Millichope for her vision and work on what really is an INCREDIBLY SMASHING cover!

To Sarah Cronin and Will Steele also for their wonderful squeal-worthy insides; they are a thing of beauty.

The dynamo that is Fiona Sharp, bookseller extraordinaire – your support for me as an author has meant so much. I am so lucky you work in Durham! You are incredible – thank you.

Gavin Hetherington, thank you also for your support and for bringing so much joy and fun to the online book world.

Jo Boyles at the wonderful Rocketship Bookshop in Salisbury and Helen Tamblyn at the equally wonderful The Barrister in Wonderland in Retford, thank you so much for getting behind me and helping to get my books out into the world.

To my AMAZING school, St Margaret's! Thank you to Helen Tait and Chloe Black for your support and to White Class – you guys are the reason I skip into work. I am so lucky to be your teacher! And to my Book Penpals and their teachers, Chris Youles, Richard Simpson and Ally Lead at East Preston Junior School, Summerfields Primary and Brookside Primary, thank you for inspiring me. Through our interactions I am always reminded what writing for kids is truly about.

To the online teacher army: Ben Harris, Scott Evans, Emily Weston (total babe), Dean Boddington, Jacqui Sydney, Kate Heap, Kevin Cobane, Jon Biddle, Miss Cleveland, Mrs Darlington, Andrew Rough, John Hughes, Jen O'Brien, Valda Varadinek, Sam Fuller, Beth Rowe, Miss Gibson and so many others, huge thanks for the amazing job you all do getting books into kids' hands.

To my agent, Sam Copeland, who probably hasn't read this far down to see his acknowledgement but here it is anyway, I don't know how you manage to do all that you do – you are quite remarkable, and thank you for managing me so brilliantly.

And look out for Jenny Pearson's next
adventure, packed with heart and humour...

GRANDPA FRANK'S GREAT BIG BUCKET LIST

Life's been a bit tricky for eleven-year-old Frank.
His dad, Frank Senior, is always in trouble, and his mum
is spending all her time at the tennis club.
But when Frank receives an inheritance of £462,000
from the grandma he didn't know he had,
things take a turn for the unexpected.

The money also comes with strict instructions
for Frank to look after his grandfather...
His very grumpy old grandfather.

But this isn't going to stop Frank!
Because he's decided to make a list of all the
things he wants to try with his grandfather.
And who ever said an eighty-year-old
can't try parkour?

COMING SOON